CRAB BAIT

Carrie Enge

ISBN: 1517321425
ISBN 13: 9781517321420

PREFACE

About twenty years ago Sue Paulsen, good friend and high school librarian, made a harmless comment: "Someone needs to write a mystery set in Petersburg." *Crab Bait* is my attempt at that mystery. I hope you will enjoy the plot, but, more importantly, I hope you will savor the setting.

To those of you who have been so supportive, I can't thank you enough.

In memory of

Ben Bunge,
the creator of the great potato sling-shot.
Laughter followed him into every room.

and

Rory Smith,
who lived on Rory Lane.
He was sweet, kindhearted, and thoughtful.

SATURDAY, MAY 17

*Our homes are here and it is not safe for anybody with
a murderer running loose.*

*Letter to the Editor
from Friends of Sing Lee
Petersburg Press, 1932*

9:00 P

Nels Dagsen's boots thumped hollowly on the board street.
This spot, where Sing Lee Alley met Chief John Lott Street,
was the oldest part of town and was a Tlingit fish camp for
centuries, until the Norwegians came and replaced the fish camp,
first with the local theater and skating rink, and then with a bar—
long, narrow and unpainted like an ersatz Tlingit long house. Homes
had been reborn as liquor stores, gas stations, cafes and the mortuary.

Nels didn't notice the smell of low tide from the harbor just a
block away—the harbor that had witnessed Tlingit landing parties
less than a hundred years ago. Those elegant red cedar canoes had
been displaced by the curved, yellow cedar planks of the Norwegian
halibut schooners. Finally, those gentle schooners had been over-
thrown by fiberglass hulls and GM diesel engines affectionately called
screaming jimmies.

Nels' own fiberglass boat was the cause of his current preoccupation. He was planning some changes—changes that would make him a few enemies and a whole lot of money if he could just keep things quiet until Thursday. On Thursday, it would all be over.

It was full daylight, only nine o'clock Alaskan time, and for a brief second the low sun broke through the clouds, glaring on wet weeds and puddles and turning the snow on Petersburg Mountain a blinding white. Shiny skunk cabbage leaves the size of small children scented the air with mustard as Dagsen continued his uneasy walk past a pile of derelict crab pots, his favorite hiding place when he was a child.

Some people said old Sing Lee, the Chinese grocer murdered in the '30s, still haunted this part of the alley; Dagsen and his childhood friends had thrilled to games of Sing Lee tag here every summer. If "Sing Lee" tagged you, you screamed "Bloody Murder" and stood frozen—dead—until you were tagged again. That scream, like the cry of a hunted animal, laced the game with dread, and Nels could remember nights when he ran home terrified, sure that Sing Lee was chasing him with a cleaver.

A strong, east wind carried a sudden downpour and the sound of accordion music from the Sons of Norway Hall less than a block away. Approaching footsteps created a steady thump on the alley's wooden planks. As Nels turned to take the shortcut down Stadsvold Trail, he heard an agitated shout behind him.

"Hey! I think you should have this." The breathless pursuer grabbed the wool of Nels' sleeve and held up a weathered Tlingit halibut hook.

Dagsen's initial impulse was to jerk his sleeve free, but when he saw the ancient, y-shaped object his anger turned to disbelief. Fissures and cracks marred the gray surface, and the stiff, spruce root twine crumbled as Dagsen took the hook.

"Are you crazy or just stupid?" Nels sputtered. Years ago his father had found this ancient Tlingit relic, the Raven Hook, and donated it to the local museum. "This is priceless. It needs to be in climate control."

"You're so concerned about important things like fishing gear and climate control that you don't have a second to worry about little things like human lives. You've taken everything that meant anything to me. You've destroyed my life, but that doesn't bother you." The voice rose with each statement. "You really are a bastard." The left hand, pulling a gun from the jacket pocket, shook in concert with the fiddlehead fronds trembling in the downpour.

Dagsen laughed. "You don't even know how to use that! Look at yourself! You're shaking too hard to even shoot." Derision turned to surprise as the first shot shattered his sternum. He spent the last millisecond of his life wondering how word of his plan had gotten out, and then a second shot knocked Nels Dagsen into the weeds at the side of Stadsvold Trail, clutching the halibut hook like a severed lifeline.

The air smelled salty as the tide began its flood. The rain's soft patter added an element of serenity to the night. The shooter hurried toward the Middle Harbor as blood eddied gracefully, tinting the puddles a delicate pink.

SUNDAY, MAY 18

If of thy mortal goods thou art bereft,
And from thy slender store,
But two loaves left,
Sell one of them, and with the dole
Buy hyacinths to soothe thy soul.

Muslihuddin Sadi
Thirteenth-Century Persian Poet

5:00 A

Dan Fields could be impatient on the best of days, and today was not the best of days. He spent half the night trying to protect Nels Dagsen's murder scene from the rain, then he came home for a quick nap, tossed for an hour listening to the rain pound on his roof, and when a pair of ravens began their rhythmic rebuke of his shiftless behavior, he decided to get up.

He gazed out his second-story window at the gray morning, the fog nestled against the mountains, the tiniest sliver of Wrangell Narrows. Usually he loved the way the rain draped the hemlocks behind his home. One morning they were army green with a shroud of gray, the next they were a sage cocoon. Every moment offered a different view from his bedroom window. But today the rain hampered Nels Dagsen's murder investigation, and Dan wanted it gone.

Well, Nels, I suspect you finally got what you deserved, he thought as he headed for the kitchen. It felt wrong, this cold heartedness. He knew a police officer should feel a little bit of empathy for the victim, but Dan wasn't hypocritical. Of all the 3,200 people in town, Nels was the only one whose death wouldn't cause him any grief. Dan knew too many stories about Nels' abuse. He was anxious to catch the murderer, he was driven to do his job, but Nels was a bastard —had been since they were children—and Dan was incapable of forgetting it.

Dan's lack of sympathy didn't pose the main problem to the investigation, though. Lilly Dagsen, Nels' sister, was the main problem. At some point Dan would have to question her, and that was something worth avoiding. He'd have to act professional, indifferent, distant. He could do that, but could she? They hadn't spoken since he left for boot camp over twenty years ago, and now he was going to casually waltz in and start grilling her about a murder investigation. How was she going to take that? She'd refused to even speak to him for two decades; it was hard to imagine she'd just start chatting it up after all this time.

Man, when did I become that kind of person? he wondered. More concerned about talking to an old girlfriend than finding a murderer? He wasn't afraid of the investigation, he'd enjoy the challenge, but the thought of dealing with Lilly had kept him obsessing since he heard about her brother's death.

He added water to the coffeemaker, slid the pot on the burner, and opened the reservoir, scalding his hand in the process. Boat coffee—water, coffee grounds and an eggshell—had been his beverage of choice, but his ex-wife Emily had broken him of that habit. Now she was gone, and she'd left nothing behind but the coffeemaker to torture him.

The coffee maker annoyed Dan, but the fact that it annoyed him also annoyed him. And the fact that he didn't just chuck it and start drinking boat coffee again annoyed him even more. He supposed the brewer was just a small symptom of the entire marriage. Maybe that was why he kept the reminder around.

He considered recusing himself from Nels Dagsen's case. Was investigating a former fiancée even ethical? Dan and Lilly hadn't been formally engaged, but they'd started talking about marriage when they were children. He couldn't just tell the chief he needed to be taken off the case because he and Lilly Dagsen had started planning their wedding when they were nine. The chief was pissy enough last night; there was no telling what kind of mood he'd be in today.

In spite of the investigation and the chief's foul mood, Dan continued obsessing about Lilly Dagsen. Man, that woman can carry a grudge, he thought as he grabbed his jacket and headed out the door.

Dan's house was "out the road." That had been his wife's idea, too. The only idea worse than the coffee pot. She didn't like those old Norwegian houses in town; they didn't have enough closet space, the stairs were too steep. She'd begged and cajoled and threatened and negotiated until he finally built a home on Rory's Lane at Papke's Landing. A few years later, she packed up and left him dealing with a twenty-five minute drive to the police station. Last night it took the chief and Sy about two minutes to get to the crime scene, but it took Dan almost half an hour.

Dan slid into his '82 Chevy and patted the dashboard, a ritual he performed every time he got behind the wheel. He'd bought the truck with his fishing settlement when he was sixteen years old, and it was stolen a few months later. Granted, he'd left the keys in the ignition, but everyone did that. The town was on an island; no one ever stole a vehicle. They didn't have anyplace to take it. But Dan's truck had disappeared for years.

Then, right after his wife left, Dan read about a Chevy S-15 in the Juneau want ads. It had the slant-six engine and everything, so he bought it on a whim. When the truck arrived on the barge, the VIN numbers matched his first vehicle. He hired the local mechanic to get it back on the road and had treated Big Red like a long, lost friend ever since.

The fifteen-mile drive from Dan's home to the police station started with several miles of muskeg marsh—a peat bog dotted with ponds and stunted evergreens. The road meandered in and out of forests, marshes and patches of fog until it settled along the edge of Wrangell Narrows, one of the world's most difficult passages to navigate, and guided travelers into the town of Petersburg, Alaska.

Everything was built on the water, and during the last mile of the drive, Dan passed two salmon canneries, a cold storage, the ferry terminal, the oil dock, one grocery store, a couple of hardware stores, the city offices, the shipwright, the library. Half-million dollar homes buttressed their pristine lawns against shipping containers and oil tanks. Zoning laws, like everything in this town, were based on fishing needs.

But Dan couldn't get his mind off Lilly. She couldn't possibly be the murderer. She and Nels had been estranged for years, but a woman like Lilly didn't just turn into a murderer. Of course, what did he know? People changed a lot after high school. She certainly managed to give him a pretty good dose of the stink eye when he saw her. But still, there was a big difference between stink eye and murder. Lilly wasn't capable of murder. He was sure of it.

Dan clutched the steering wheel with impatience and glanced in the rearview mirror. Brows that angled up in constant surprise bracketed a crooked nose, creating a hobbit-meets-professional-wrestler look. His short, muscular body had been out of place on the basketball court, and, years ago, when a woman wrote a letter to the editor about the need for a bulwark to keep cars from overshooting Hungry Point curve, Dan's basketball coach had jokingly suggested the city use Dan. He'd taken the ribbing good-naturedly. He was one of those rare people who could dish it out and take it.

The diesel generators rumbled as he rounded the final curve into town. Saturday was the last full day of the Little Norway Festival and Dan had worried that a wayward drunk might amble onto the crime scene, but the protective canopy was still intact. Unfortunately, Stadsvold Trail looked like a ditch running from Main Street to Sing Lee Alley. As he drove past the murder scene to the coffee shop, he wondered how they'd ever find footprints in that muck.

The Pastime Café had been the heart of the town for generations, and dusty flower arrangements were the only attempt at renovation. Worn gray linoleum, pocked yellow walls and florescent lighting didn't add to the ambience, but the heavy wooden barstools were smooth and solid and comforting to slide onto.

Low Floatin' Johnny Stadsvold sat on one of these barstools, hugging his coffee mug like he was trying to inhale peace from its steamy warmth. Anyone who didn't know he'd discovered Nels' body the night before would think a hangover was the cause of his hunched shoulders and bloodshot eyes.

"Hey, Low Floatin'," Dan said. Neither man had to signal the waitress; Doris had heard about the murder and hovered around the two men, topping off mugs. She bobbed and darted toward them like a sparrow searching for that tiny crumb to take home to her nest.

Dan, sitting in a hunched stance similar to Johnny's, considered the contrasts between Nels Dagsen, the murdered seiner, and Low Floatin' Johnny, the gillnetter who discovered his body.

Southeast Alaska has three main types of commercial salmon fishers. Trollers are the elitists; they extend several lines from long poles off the sides of the boat. When they catch a fish, it's brought on board in pristine condition. Trollers may not catch a lot of fish, but the fish they catch are firm, silver and perfect in every way, and they get top dollar for them.

The seiners hunker at the opposite end of the food chain. Seiners pull a huge net around schools of fish, purse the bottom closed and haul thousands of fish out of the water in one set. Because of the weight of the fish pressing against the purse seine and each other, seine fish can be misshapen by the time they reach the processors. Seiners deal with quantity over quality, but when the fishing is good, there is plenty of money for the skipper and the four or five man crew.

A gillnetter, or fish strangler, rolls one or two or three hundred fathoms of fine, spider web-like net off the stern of the boat. The salmon swim into the net, and when they try to back out, their gills catch in the web, trapping or "gilling" the fish. Not as many fish are caught, but they are usually only damaged around the head and gills, so the gillnetters get a better price for their fish than the seiners.

Trollers, the environmentalists of the fleet, take pride in the pristine quality of their catch. Seiners, the high rollers of the fleet, may be nursing high blood pressure and ulcers, but they take pride in their large houses on the water in Petersburg and their large houses on the golf course in Palm Springs. Gillnetters are the independents of the fleet. They take pride in the quality of their catch, but their main concern is that they don't have to spend days out fishing to catch a few hundred fish like the trollers, and they don't have to deal with an ill-trained, hung-over crew like the seiners.

Nels Dagsen had been a seiner, aggressive and gregarious with money to spare. Johnny Stadsvold was a gillnetter, and he liked to lay low. For the last thirty or forty years he had been plugging away on his gillnetter, the *Lofoten, or Low Floatin'* as people who didn't speak Norwegian called it, and living in the family apartment building on Sing Lee Alley. When Dan was in elementary school, he had watched Low Floatin' play basketball, and his fishing and basketball strategies were similar—work hard, keep your head, and play it safe.

"I'm surprised you're up so early. You had a heck of a night," Dan said.

"No shit. I keep seeing Nels lying in all that skunk cabbage with his eyes wide open. I used to take that trail home from the bar just about every night, but never again." Johnny's wiry frame gave a tiny shiver; the gray in his beard seemed more noticeable than it was the night before. "The creepiest thing was the raven on that halibut hook. I swear to god, it looked just like Nels. It had this surprised look on its little face." He took another gulp of coffee and then, after a pause added, "You know what else I've been thinking about? I screwed up last night. I didn't tell the chief that *Tlingit Pride* guy from Kake was at the bar when I went back. After I found Nels."

"*Tlingit Pride* guy? You mean Marvin Brown? Are you shitting me Johnny?"

"I shit you not. He wasn't there at first, but after I found Nels and went back, he was sitting at the table with the guys."

Dan couldn't believe this new information. Marvin Brown, a resident of the village of Kake, had all kinds of reasons to want Nels out of the way. Nels' steel boat, the *Norge,* had rammed the wooden *Tlingit Pride* during a herring opening the previous spring. The "accident" had cost Marvin a huge load of herring and valuable fishing time.

Since Marvin lived in Kake, a village that filled a full page and a half in the phone book and was located on the other side of Kupreanof Island, he wouldn't normally be a suspect, but his presence in Petersburg made a huge difference. Maybe the murder would be resolved faster than Dan thought. At the very least, Dan might interview Marvin Brown while someone else talked to Lilly Dagsen. The dark cloud that had been following him all morning lifted at the thought of avoiding Lilly.

"So you got a theory on all this?" Dan asked.

"Hell, I've got theories on everything, but nobody ever listens to them. I mean, Nels wasn't the most popular guy at the polka, was he? What about that old couple he abandoned in Dixon Entrance?"

Nels' crewmen told a story about a run from Seattle to a herring opening south of Ketchikan in unusually warm weather. The Fish and Game started talking about opening the fishery earlier than Nels had anticipated. The crew was pushing the boat hard when a thirty-six foot cruiser radioed for help. The engine was down and they were trying to run with a seven-horse kicker. They expected the Coast Guard in a few hours, but in the meantime they were stuck in the middle of Dixon Entrance.

Nels told them they were fine and continued on to the herring opening where the *Norge* had one good set that netted each crewman an $8,200 crewshare before they headed back to Petersburg. Days later they heard that the weather had turned snotty, the Coast Guard hadn't made it in time, and the cruiser had gone down. Supposedly Nels' only comment was, "Why do we pay taxes for the Coast Guard if they can't do their job?"

"You should probably question his whole crew," Low Floatin' added. "He screws them on their crew shares every year. That first opening last summer, Nels' skiff man said they had one set of about ten thousand pounds of sockeyes, but I just don't see that happening. Last summer was a cold one, and you know the fish run later when the summer's cold."

"No, the only thing I know is how every conversation with you works its way around to fish talk," Dan said, slapping Low Floatin' on the back and heading toward the door.

"Sometimes we talk basketball," Johnny said to Dan's retreating backside, but Dan had already forgotten Low Floatin' Johnny Stadsvold. His mind had moved on to Marvin Brown. Things were looking up. He knew Lilly wouldn't kill her brother.

7:00 A

By the time Dan reached the police station, the entire town had heard at least one version of the murder—some had heard three or four. Rumors were airborne, a lot like different strains of a virus. The Lutheran congregation would circulate the Lute strain, *Lutefisk sacrilegious,* attributing the crime to "an outsider." Some of the churchgoers would have a truly Christian attitude about the crime and some would silently believe that Nels deserved everything he got, but regardless of the individual's perspective, Nels and Lilly would be added to the prayer chain.

The Forest Service strain of the rumor, *Pulpus hypocriticus,* would spread like wildfire. Most of the Forest Service professionals wouldn't really know much about Nels, so they would limit their comments to community safety, saying something like "I moved my family to Alaska to avoid crime, and now someone's gone and got murdered right on the path I take to the office. I'm thinking about transferring the family to Portland." Then they would discuss the possibility of regulating murder in specific areas of the country.

The Harbor Bar strain, *Rainier inebriata,* would originate with the story told by Johnny Stadsvold. Then it would meander and oscillate and sometimes even stagger, depending on the blood alcohol level of the individual discussing the event, until poor Nels was gutted, dismembered, and reassembled a lot like the salmon nuggets currently being promoted by the local fish industry. In spite of the sobering topic, the Harbor Bar version would end with someone ringing the bell to buy a round in Nels' honor. Since there wasn't usually more than a handful of people in the bar at one time, it was a frugal investment on a grand gesture.

Dan considered the potential for creative rumors as he walked into the chief's office. It was the only room in the police department with a window, but the chief always kept the shades down. A florescent blue-white glare cast angular shadows on Sy Haube, Dan's friend and fellow police officer; Arne, the weekend dispatcher; and the chief, who were all staring down at the Tlingit halibut hook centered on the polished desktop.

"Look at that thing," the chief said. The group studied the weathered, twelve-inch, wooden *y*; a stylized Tlingit raven was carved into the long side. The broken beak separated large, ovoid eyes with concave centers, and the claws looked disturbingly like tiny human hands. "God knows how long it sat in the rain last night. It's falling apart, and we'll be taking the heat for that. We've got enough to do without dealing with that thing." The chief, jutting his chin toward the offending hook, gave his desktop a quick slap. "It's priceless. That's all I've heard from anyone. It's priceless. No one's concerned about the dead guy. All anyone's talking about is that damn hook." He leaned in for a closer look and then shoved himself away from his desk. "I swear the thing's disintegrating before my eyes."

The chief's foul mood permeated the group as they discussed the investigation. First there was the evidence. Not only had it been raining last night when the body was reported, it had been raining for two solid days before the discovery and was still raining this morning. The only difference was that at about the time of the discovery, almost as if by plan, the rain had intensified. Stadsvold Trail didn't have many decent surfaces for footprints on a good day, and now most of it was two inches under water. Then there was the sheer number of partial footprints. Since the Fish-o-Rama was held at the nearby Sons of Norway Hall the night before, half the participants had probably slogged down that trail last evening.

"We can't afford to make even the tiniest mistake on this case or we'll get eaten alive, and to be perfectly honest, I've never run a murder investigation before. I'm not even sure where to start. I called Juneau and they're sending down a hotshot to help us out," the chief said. His chair sounded like a nerve-splintering foghorn as he scooted it forward. "We've got three guys to deal with a priceless antique and a murder."

"Has the hotshot worked anyplace besides Juneau?" Dan asked.

"No, and I know what you're thinking. Juneau isn't exactly murder capital of the world, but they've had three murders in the last five years, and this guy's worked on all three of them. The Juneau chief says he's a real go-getter, like a wolverine when he gets started on something."

"We can use the help," Dan said. "We don't seem to have much else going for us."

"Where the hell have you been?" the chief focused on Dan.

"I've been talking to Low Floatin' Johnny. He forgot to tell you Marvin Brown was at the bar last night."

"Well, that's something, anyway. We'll need to talk to Marvin; so far we don't have much to go on."

No one had heard a thing. The few people who lived near the trail had bailed out to avoid the noise of the band at Sons or Norway or to go to the Fish-o-Rama. Then, there was the matter of the victim. People wouldn't openly express dislike for Nels Dagsen, a local boy who was a good ball handler and a good fisherman. He had been willing to chat and charm if he thought someone was worth cultivating. But there were a lot of rumors about Nels' past—a whole lot of skeletons in his fish hold.

"What about DNA?" Dan asked.

"I don't know about the DNA. It depends on how long that damn hook was in the rain. It's so delicate, no one wants me to ship it to Anchorage, but we can't do DNA here. I'd send it up with one of you guys, but I can't spare you." He ran his fingers through his hair and then scooted his chair back, slamming into the wall. "I want that thing off my desk before something happens to it. I'll deal with getting the hook out of town. Dan, you go interview Lilly Dagsen, and Sy, see if you can find Marvin Brown." The chief's bushy gray brows cast a shadow that made his eyes look hollow.

Dan could feel his face redden as he spoke. "I was thinking maybe I'd better interview Marvin, and Sy can interview Lilly." The chief's face hardened in stubborn opposition, but the ringing phone interrupted his response, leaving Dan to contemplate the pending interview with a woman he disliked and distrusted, and the pending storm with his boss who was in a flagrantly foul mood.

As the phone conversation progressed, the chief punctuated *uh-huhs* and *I know thats* with agitated drawer slamming and chair scraping. "That twine was coming loose before we even saw it," he said as he pinched the bridge of his nose. "What you don't seem to understand is that I'm investigating a murder, and unless someone hands me a legal document that says otherwise, the murder takes priority over old fishing gear." He slammed down the receiver and the room went into an anxious state of suspended animation. Time hovered for a few silent moments until the chief turned to Dan. "Listen, Dan, I hired you because I thought you'd do what needs to get done, not because I thought you'd argue with me every time I give orders. Everybody is looking at us right now. Understand? Everybody. When people are watching us this close, you don't even think about doing your own thinking."

Dan and Sy headed for the door as the chief shouted, "I want you *both* there to interview Lilly Dagsen and you can *both* track down Marvin Brown." Turning to the dispatcher he said, "Arne, get the State Museum curator. At home if you need to. And screen my calls. Especially my wife."

"What the hell just happened?" Dan said.

"Sounds like his wife blind-sided him about the halibut hook last night, and the phone drove him out of the house this morning. It's got him worried," Sy explained as the two walked to Lilly's apartment across from the hardware store. The chief's wife had never liked Petersburg. She didn't feel welcome, she didn't fit in. So the chief hadn't worried about job security: if he got canned, his wife would be happy to move. But now, with his wife serving on the church council and chairing the quilting guild, she wanted to stay. Now the chief worried about job security.

Dan shook his head. "Why is he taking it out on us, anyway?"

"I don't think he's taking it out on us, I think he's taking it out on you," Sy said with a smile. "He took some heat when he hired you, but he wasn't worried about it then. He didn't figure you'd screw up, and if you did, the worse that could happen, he'd get fired and his wife would be happy they could leave town. But now if you screw up, he'll get fired and his wife won't be happy."

"I'm going back to talk to him."

"Ohhhh, no you're not." Sy grabbed Dan's arm and walked him in the opposite direction. "That's exactly what he's worried about: that you'll fly off the handle. Besides, he did go out on a limb to hire you, but now isn't the time to discuss it. Now is the time to be a team player and prove his decision was a good one."

"Did you see his eyebrows?" Dan asked. "They were defying all laws of gravity." Both men laughed. They shared a theory that they could tell the extent of the chief's foul mood by how tightly his eyebrows curled.

Sy, a tall, slim, wide-shouldered Native with short black hair and laugh lines at the corners of his dark eyes, had spent most of his childhood in the neighboring town of Wrangell. He and Dan had been good friends since their senior year of high school when Sy moved to Petersburg to play ball for his uncle, the coach. Although Dan had never asked, he suspected Sy had helped him get his job at the department. And it had worked out well; they made a good team. Sy liked the meticulous, analytical side of police work, so he did the fingerprinting and more detailed tasks. Dan, the impetuous local boy, liked the social side of police work, so he did the interviews and the mingling.

Sy kept Dan grounded, and at this point Dan knew he was right. There was too much going on. "Everybody's got stock in that halibut hook," Sy said. "The chief's answering to every anthropologist, art lover, and Native group in Alaska, and you saw it—it's falling apart. He's trying to solve a murder, but instead he has to babysit a priceless antique that happens to be our only piece of evidence."

9:00 A

Dan and Sy quickly reached the long flight of stairs leading to Lilly's apartment. Lilly had placed a half barrel of red tulips and white hyacinths at the foot of the steps. A piece of green, monofilament gillnet was stretched over a skeleton of PVC pipe to keep the deer away from the flowers. A rusty oil tank and decaying wooden stairs created an unsettling contrast to the cheerful planter. The steps bowed and swayed under Dan's physical weight while his thoughts bowed and swayed under the mental weight of a meeting with Lilly Dagsen. "You do the talking, Sy."

"Come on, Dan, you can handle an ex-girlfriend after twenty years," Sy said as he knocked on the unpainted door.

"Yeah, it's just that this particular ex-girlfriend still gives me soul-freezing hate stares." Dan considered Lilly, Nels' only sibling, as they waited at her door. She probably could have killed Nels and gotten off with justifiable homicide. He had been torpedoing her life for decades. At the end of their junior year of high school, Lilly's dad had died and left Nels the boat to fish as long as he wanted. Once it was sold, the money generated from the sale was to be split between Nels and Lilly. The thing Old Man Dagsen hadn't taken into consideration was the limited entry proposal that Alaska's Department of Fish and Game was implementing to control the salmon fishery. The proposal limited fishing to people with permits, and to get a permit, someone had to have fished in a specific fishery for the last several years.

Old Man Dagsen qualified for a number of different permits, but since the law hadn't been finalized, and he was opposed to any government regulations, he hadn't mentioned what should happen to his permits. Everyone agreed they would have to stay with the boat for Nels to continue fishing, so initially the question was irrelevant. Then the permits started increasing in value, and within a few years the licenses that were originally free sold for a quarter million dollars or more. So while her brother turned the commercial fishing bubble of the eighties into a life of prosperity—millions of dollars worth of prosperity—Lilly Dagsen lived in an apartment over the drugstore

When Lilly opened her peeling and weathered apartment door, it was hard to imagine she was heir to a virtual kingdom.

"Hey." Lilly, slim with bobbed, blonde hair and wide-set eyes, hugged Sy as the two men entered the kitchen. She had aged overnight, but if you ignored the tiny lines around her eyes, she still looked like a middle-schooler.

"Sorry about Nels," Sy said.

Rather than responding, Lilly focused on the two men who had started pulling off their rubber boots.

"Don't bother about those," she said, but the comment was just a formality. She knew they would take off their boots and waited until they were in stocking feet to lead them through the kitchen and into the cave-like, brown paneled living room. In spite of the half-open window, the heat stifled Dan who could hear traffic passing on the wet pavement below.

As Dan sat in an overstuffed couch that had been dark green velvet in high school, a wave of nostalgia engulfed him. He remembered all of the furniture and even many of the pictures in the room from Lilly's parents' house. "Are you holding up okay, Lilly?"

"I almost skipped church." Lilly directed her response to Sy. "I'm so glad I decided to go. Everyone was sweet, supportive. Food's already stacking up in the kitchen." She sat on the piano bench looking at her feet. The stark white blouse of her Norwegian dress ruffled around her throat and washed out her creamy complexion.

"Sorry we have to bother you at a time like this," Sy said.

"I knew you'd be coming. I've been worrying about how to act. That's kind of unnatural, isn't it?" Pink hives crept up her neck as she spoke. "Your brother dies and instead of grieving for him, you worry about how you should behave. I'm afraid everyone is watching me for signs I'm happy about his murder." Lilly leaned back against the upright piano that had been her mother's.

When Dan was eight or nine, he helped move that old piano into the Dagsens' living room. He always helped Lilly and her mom: tightening Lilly's bike chain, picking slugs off her mother's flowers. That was part of the reason he spent so much time at the Dagsens'. Lilly's mom always needed him, and he liked being needed.

Sy's cell phone buzzed, leaving Dan and Lilly in a strained silence that started Dan pacing. The room was too warm by the kitchen and too cold by the window. He inspected a bevy of family pictures including one familiar print of a picnic at the Smiccum Club. He'd been there for that picture. He should have been on the left with a bucket of tadpoles, but his side of the photo was folded under. Instead, a beaming Lilly sat by herself, elbows awry, curls in a tumbling blonde halo. Her hair was straighter now. When did that happen? he wondered. When do women's curls go straight? And, for that matter, when had the sweet, carefree girl in the picture turned into this rigid, jaded woman?

Minutes slogged until Sy returned. "Sounds like someone broke into the Fishing Co-op Hardware store last night. A gun's missing. The chief wants me to start working the prints, and you're supposed to find out anything you can about the halibut hook. Oh, yeah, and question Marvin Brown."

Lilly walked Sy to the door and returned silently to the piano bench.

"Sorry about Nels," Dan said, and then mentally kicked himself. She'd just said she didn't know how to act and here he was putting her on the spot. "I was hoping Sy could question you," and then he gave himself a second mental kick.

"Well, this is one of life's great ironies. The first time in twenty years I speak with my long, lost best friend, and he's treating me like a murder suspect. Who'd imagine it would come to this?"

His initial thought was to waspishly remind her that she caused the awkward position, but he fought the urge and stuck to the investigation. "You're not a suspect, Lilly. We're just looking for background information on Nels.

"I know your dad found the Raven Hook up Petersburg Creek. It was the summer I was fishing in the Bay. How did it wind up at the museum?"

"Dad and Nels had a huge argument about it. It was one of the few times I ever heard them disagree. My dad wanted to donate it to the Petersburg Museum and Nels wanted it on loan to the State Museum."

"That doesn't seem like anything worth fighting about."

"It was for them. Dad wanted it in Petersburg so everyone would think of him as the swell guy who found a valuable artifact and donated it to their museum. Nels wanted it in climate control at the State Museum so it wouldn't deteriorate, and he could sell it as soon as dad died." She bit a nail thoughtfully and then continued. "When Dad died, Nels tried to get me to go in with him and get a lawyer. He wanted to get the hook back from the museum, and sell it to the Smithsonian." She avoided eye contact with Dan as she spoke. "Nels and my dad were these huge powerful forces, and now they're both gone. It seems impossible."

Lilly arranged the pictures on the piano, nudging a print of her father toward the back as if the family was losing relevance as she spoke. "For most of the town the hook was an icon —almost a religious relic, like a piece of the true cross or something—but for my dad and Nels, it was nothing but a way to promote their own interests."

"Can you think of any reason Nels would have the Raven Hook last night?"

"No, I can't believe Nels would even touch the hook. He knew how fragile it was. That was why he always said it should be in the State Museum. Under climate control. Nels was all about the climate control. He liked everything frigid. And controlled."

Dan examined the philodendron growing in water on the coffee table and realized a gold fish was swimming among the roots. Lilly had brought her own little eco-system into her shabby apartment. He felt a little like the fish—under water, weaving through a tangle. He needed to organize his questions, but old memories kept getting in his way. "So, what was Nels' last wife's name? Mary or something? I don't suppose you know how I could contact her?"

"Her name's Meera and she'll be in on tomorrow's jet."

"She's coming for his funeral?"

"No. She's coming to talk to a lawyer. They're still married."

"So the money all goes to Meera?"

"No, Dan, half of it's mine. That's what Dad's will stipulated. Meera and I will split it."

"If you'd taken him to court when he was still alive, things would be a lot easier now, you know."

"Well, that's a new angle. I didn't realize part of your job as a police officer was to give financial advice to next of kin."

"I'm sorry, Lilly, I've just watched you for all these years —."

"You shouldn't have been watching me, you had a wife to watch."

He walked to the window and looked at the street below. Swede Gunderson was heading out of Knudsen & Holtan's, "Hardware, House Wares, Gifts and Lumber," when he ran into one of his deckhands carrying a dirty oil filter. They were having an animated discussion in the middle of the street, the deckhand occasionally flinging an arc of oil as he gestured with the filter. A pick-up driver waited until they finished their conversation and then drove on. That was what he loved about this little town: that comfortable sense of community. And this morning it was crumbling—for him and Lilly and even for the chief.

"Who else might want Nels dead?"

Lilly recited a litany of relationships. There were the divorces— several of them. Nels had married a local girl, his childhood sweetheart, right out of high school. She put him through college in more ways than one: working to pay the rent and tuition, writing most of his papers, and even taking some of his tests. Then, immediately after graduation, Nels dumped her like toxic waste.

He brought a nineteen-year-old up from San Francisco; the locals weren't impressed with her avant garde clothing and big city attitude, but they didn't have to tolerate her for long. She was gone in less than a year. After that, there was a summer with a high school student working on Nels' boat, the *Norge*.

And then he started seriously shopping around. He went to Russia and brought home a gorgeous nineteen year old who barely spoke English and walked to town in her leather coat and tall, high-heeled boots—the most impractical foul weather gear the locals had ever seen. She lasted a couple of years before he traded her in on a new model, a petite, dazzling Philippina who disappeared a few years ago and hadn't been replaced. And to complicate matters, each of the marriages had been punctuated with several short flings with women of every conceivable ethnicity, age, and income bracket.

"Lofloten' Johnny was telling me about a broke-down cruiser Nels left in Dixon Entrance? Do you know anything about that?" Dan asked.

"That story isn't true. The crew circulated it because Nels shorted them on their crew share. My brother might have been a bastard, but he wasn't a monster. Come on, Dan."

Dan had tiptoed through the questioning and Lilly was still bitter. He decided to quit trying to be delicate and just finish. "Where were you last night from about seven until about nine thirty?"

"There's the question I've been waiting for. 'Where were you on the night of the murder?'"

"You're not a suspect, Lilly, but we still have to rule you out."

"That makes no sense at all."

"Where were you?"

"I was at Sons of Norway. Serving at the dinner and then cleaning up." The pink blotches on her neck darkened to magenta as she spoke.

"Can anyone verify that you didn't leave Sons of Norway?"

"For not being a suspect, I sure feel like one." She walked into the kitchen, leaving Dan to follow. "I don't have time for this. I have friends coming over for lunch."

"Are you serious? Your brother just got murdered and you're having friends over?"

"You don't know about funerals, Officer. I do. I've planned a few. And now I am planning another one, and I need some help." She filled a tall stockpot with water and added a handful of salt as she spoke. "Or does planning your brother's funeral move you higher up on the suspect list? Oh, that's right. I'm not even on the suspect list."

"Let's try this again. Is there anyone who can verify that you didn't leave Sons of Norway last night?"

Lilly let the question hover as she tore open a plastic bag of shrimp and dumped them in the sink. "Nancy Goodman and I were working together. We served for a while and then we went out to the gazebo to cool down. That was it."

The gazebo, part of the Bojer Wikan Fishermen's Memorial to Petersburg fishers lost at sea, was right next to the Sons of Norway.

"And Nels was at the dinner?"

"I think we already went over this." Her back to Dan, she sorted shrimp as she spoke.

"No, I don't think we did." Dan could barely keep his voice even. "What time was Nels at the dinner?"

"I don't know. He walked around slapping asses for about ten minutes and then left as far as I could tell."

"What time?"

"We were busy. The Viking Mobile pulled up, and things got crazy."

"Look, we're not playing a game. What time was Nels at the dinner?"

"Maybe our friendship didn't last, but you still know my history better than anyone else. Do you actually expect me to pretend to be upset about Nels? That would be hypocritical, even by your standards."

Dan could feel heat radiating from the back of his head toward his face. The thought that Lilly might notice made him even more anxious. Maybe she hadn't changed that much on the outside, but this cold, inflexible woman was completely different from the one he had known all those years ago. "I'll stop by later today. In the meantime I want you to list anyone who can verify you didn't leave the Sons of Norway last night."

"Roger that, officer. As long as I'm not a suspect." Lilly picked up the largest, side-stripe shrimp, popped its head off, and slam-dunked the head into the trash.

10:00 A

Dan thumped down Lilly's stairs, his mind sputtering like water in a hot skillet. He had loved her so much and now, here she was, a cold, angry, hardheaded…. What did she think she was doing? She would be the prime suspect if she kept acting like this.

Hell, she should be the prime suspect anyway. Maybe she had killed her brother. Half of a fishing empire is a decent motive for anyone. And she even looked guilty. She broke out in hives and started getting defensive as soon as he asked about an alibi. They needed to take a good, close look at Lilly Dagsen instead of treating her like some special circumstance.

Dan continued thinking as he headed toward Stadsvold Trail. Shit! Was he just vindictive? Looking closer at her because of the way she treated him? Turning into that kind of cop? And why was she so pissy toward him anyway? He was the one she'd screwed around on. What gave her the right to go all righteous on him?

Stadsvold Trail was close to Sons of Norway. He needed to figure exactly how long it would take a murderer to get from Sons of Norway to the murder site at the foot of the trail. As he walked, he thought back to all the years he and Lilly had been friends. They'd been like two parts of a whole. Could someone so sweet turn into a murderer? She wouldn't pour salt on slugs when she was little, how could she kill the last surviving member of her family now?

Of course, her mother was pretty unstable. Actually, the whole family was one bead off center. And here she was having friends over for lunch less than twenty-four hours after her brother was killed. Hell, it was only about twelve hours. That was cold. And she didn't look at him when he was questioning her. She started working on those shrimp and kept her back to him, so he couldn't see her face as she worked.

If Dan told the chief that Lilly wouldn't look at him, the chief would think she was guilty for sure. Failure to make eye contact. That was a clear sign of deception. Well, so what? He wasn't protecting Lilly Dagsen anymore; she wouldn't even give him a straight answer when he was trying to do his job. He would never trust her again. He needed to wipe the old Lilly from his mind. She was gone.

As he thought, he paced off the distance from Stadsvold Trail to Sons of Norway. It took forty-three seconds to walk from the trail to the board street, over the hand made wooden speed bump—or *farts-demper,* as the Norwegian speed bump sign called it—to the Sons of Norway Hall that crouched like a loyal sentry over Hammer Slough.

Dan entered the memorial park next to the hall and leaned on a railing. Forty-three seconds to walk from the hall to the trail. Probably thirty seconds for a runner. The murderer could follow Nels from the dinner, shoot him, and be back at the dinner in three minutes and not even be out of breath.

He looked up the slough at the old cedar warehouses, their mouths wide open and waiting for fishing boats that would never return. The *Cypress* and *Silver Crest*. The *Augusta*. A cool mist settled on his cheeks and brows, calming crystals in the midst of a chaotic day. The water, greenish-brown and impenetrable, flowed out of the slough on the ebb tide.

I'll be go to hell, Dan thought as he turned and began running toward downtown. The gun's in the water. The killer shot Nels and chucked the gun in the slough. It was obvious, inevitable. The certainty of it hit him like a tiderip.

10:30 A

"Hey, Arne, is the chief busy?" Dan asked as he entered the police station.

"Yeah, he hasn't been off the phone since you guys left."

Dan entered the office and sat down. He was excited to tell the chief his theory about the gun, but the chief, leaning back in his chair, scowled and continued discussing the hook.

After several minutes of *uh-huhs* and *we can do that's*, the chief hung up and turned his bushy brows toward Dan. "I thought you were working on interviews."

"Yeah, I'll get right back to them, I wanted to talk to you about the gun. It's in the slough. I'd bet money on it. That's what I'd do with it if I shot somebody on Stadsvold Trail. I'd chuck the gun in the slough, so if I ran into anybody else, I wouldn't have it on me."

"Jeez, you're probably right about that."

"It's almost slack water now. This would be the time to look for it." Dan hoped the chief would realize the need to start searching quickly, but the chief had other thoughts.

"Have you talked to Marvin Brown yet?"

"Nope, just Lilly Dagsen."

"I want you talking to Marvin Brown. He's our best bet right now. I'll figure something out about the gun."

Even such a dark, rainy day was a bright contrast to the Harbor Bar's cave-like interior. Dan paused a beat to regain his equilibrium and walked over and sat at the bar, shooting a smile toward Yvette, the town's patron saint of underdogs and losers. Yvette had been a fixture behind that bar for years and her presence was as much of a draw as the alcohol she poured. Every man, woman and dog in Petersburg appreciated her good-natured support of anyone or anything in need.

Yvette's 280 pounds overflowed a small metal stool that looked as if it should crumple under her weight. "Don't suppose you came to propose marriage," she said.

"You know I would if I was half the man you deserve, Vette." Dan and Yvette's friendship started in their senior year of high school when they were called into the principal's office for what Yvette referred to as a security breach.

As a trusted member of the journalism class, Yvette borrowed the teacher's keys anytime she needed to work in the dark room. Dan had complained about the basketball team's limited practice time. Beyond their two-hour practices and their two weekend games, the boys were relegated to an uneven, uncovered, and unfenced cement slab with puddles that lent new meaning to the word "dribble." Yvette got a copy of the journalism teacher's keys made for the team, and they practiced for days in the gym until someone reported the group.

The principal kicked Dan and Yvette out of extra-curricular activities for the rest of the year. Yvette sat with Dan at all the basketball games, and Dan sat with Yvette when the new yearbook came out. The two had been good friends ever since, and Dan was glad she was involved in the investigation. She would be a good sounding board.

"Okay, so who is the 'long arm of the law' reaching out to throttle at this stage of the investigation?" she asked.

"Heard Marvin Brown was in town last night."

Yvette shook her head in disbelief. "You come ambling in to my bar and have the goddamn gall to suggest Marvin Brown is a murderer? Right when I'd started thinking you might be the one salvageable man in all of Southeast Alaska."

"I don't know what gave you the impression I was salvageable."

"Marvin Brown, Dan?"

"Okay, Vette, help me out here. Tell me about Marvin, so I can cross him off my very short list of suspects."

"Marvin arrived. Marvin shot the shit. Marvin left."

"That's a start. What *time* did Marvin arrive?" Dan asked.

"I don't know. I never remember what I was doing an hour ago. I noticed Marvin coming in. I think it was after Lofloatin' Johnny left, but I'm not even sure about that. I was washing glasses at the time, if that helps."

"Did he seem agitated?"

"Yeah, he was agitated." Yvette grabbed a flimsy plastic cutting board and started slicing lemons. "He'd run his boat over from Kake with a bum propeller, and it hadn't been pleasant. He was going on the grid, and he wasn't looking forward to it. Then Jack Olsen and the boys started up about what kind of zincs Marvin was going to use and telling him horror stories about zincs and propellers and boats on the grid. So, does that help any with the investigation?"

"How do you know he was just nervous about going on the grid?"

"He walked in and bought a beer. I said he looked tired, and he said the run over had been hell because the boat shimmied all the way. Then he headed for Jack's table and they started talking zincs."

"How long did they talk about the zincs? Any idea?"

"I don't know exactly, but it was quite a while. Marvin must have showed right after Johnny left because they went on about zincs for a good half hour. So does that give Marvin the proverbial 'alibi'?"

"Not really. Nels was facedown in a bunch of water so we don't have an estimated time of death yet. We're waiting to hear from Anchorage."

"I can see where time of death might be useful, but not so that you can pin a murder on Marvin Brown, Dan. I always thought you had your head on straight, but here you are investigating the sweetest guy in the fleet for murder."

"Simmer down, Vette, we don't have Marvin cuffed on death row, I'm just trying to eliminate as many suspects as I can, and I don't need to have you flipping me crap while I do it."

Dan headed toward to door. "Rocky's coming home in a few days and I plan on having this straightened out by then." He hadn't seen his youngest son, Rocky, since the boy left for Afghanistan almost a year earlier. He'd been counting the days until his son got home, and Rocky's arrival was the only thing Dan considered more important than the murder investigation.

As he reached the exit, Yvette shouted after him: "If you're in such a hurry, why don't you question Lilly Dagsen? I think she looks pretty damn good for this one."

Yvette's comment ratcheted Dan's frustration up one more notch. If people are already pointing at Lilly, wait until they find out she's having friends over for lunch, he thought, and then added, Shit, why do I even care? Evidently the chief's concern was justified. Yvette was a whole lot more caustic than he'd anticipated. A half-day into the investigation and people were making allegiances, and they weren't based on logic. They were based on how polite someone was at the bar, or when someone had friends over for lunch, or who had asked someone to the prom.

Dan was heading toward the grid when he heard the jet approaching. The Juneau hotshot would take some of the pressure off him and Sy. Maybe he could take over the search for the gun. Then he could avoid any more uncomfortable interviews with Lilly—or Yvette. But just as a swell of relief started to buoy his mood, the jet's drone turned to a roar, and he realized it was overflying. Visibility was below minimum and the jet, along with the Juneau hotshot, would be skipping Petersburg and heading to Wrangell. The footprints on Stadsvold trail were already under water. How long before they'd completely disintegrate?

Shit! He thought again as he continued toward the harbor and Marvin Brown.

11:30 A

When the town was founded, Main Street and Sing Lee Alley were right on the water, but fill had been added in the 50s and now the walk from Main Street to the harbor was an entire block long—a block Dan used to consider Marvin's situation. Was Marvin actually the type of guy who would run his boat over from Kake, shoot someone and then go have a beer? His response to the Sitka ramming had been mild, but that didn't mean he wasn't capable of murder, it just meant he wasn't the typical hotheaded herring fisherman.

The Alaskan herring roe fishery was a relatively recent phenomenon. In the 1970s, fishermen had been forced to diversify as salmon fishing became less and less lucrative. If you had a bad salmon season, you could make up for it with another fishery—say, halibut, or herring. But herring was a crapshoot. Three or four boats out of fifty would get huge sets worth thousands of dollars, and the rest of the fleet would go home hungry.

And the fishery was riddled with politics. The Fish and Game used the percentage of herring roe to determine the fishing schedule. If they opened when the herring roe was at ten per cent, the fish were worth a designated amount determined by the Japanese market, maybe $1,000 a ton. But if they waited until the percentage was, say, thirteen per cent, the herring were worth significantly more, even $1,600 a ton. The problem was, if Fish and Game waited too long, those inconsiderate herring might just go ahead and spawn without the Fish and Game's permission. Then the fishery was a total bust.

Every year a fleet of hungry seiners would head to Sitka to catch herring. Since they didn't know exactly when the fishery would open, they'd get to town early and sit around and grumble. The happily married members of the fleet liked a high percentage of roe, but they'd rather be sleeping in their own beds than worrying about a crew. The young, single, or not-so-happily married wanted to wait for a better roe percentage to make more money, or enjoy one of Southeast Alaska's few topless bars. Regardless of their intent, everyone would be spending money as if they had it. Finally, the flare would go off and an ornery group of hung-over fishermen would have fifteen minutes to make a fortune.

With the stakes so high, it wasn't surprising things often got out of hand. The *Tlingit Pride*, Marvin Brown's fifty-two foot wooden seiner, had started making a set on a huge school of herring. Nels Dagsen had his eye on the same school, but the fifty-eight foot, steel-hulled *Norge* wasn't as nimble as the *Tlingit Pride*. When Nels realized he couldn't out-maneuver the smaller boat, he rammed the *Tlingit Pride* so hard that it couldn't complete the set. Nels' steel boat crushed the wooden hull and cost Marvin Brown an eighty thousand dollar herring settlement.

First Marvin Brown got screwed out of a substantial herring set, and then he had the uncommon misfortune of stumbling smack dab into the middle of a murder investigation. At the time Nels Dagsen was shot, the *Tlingit Pride* was lying at the Middle Harbor, a quick jog down one float and a short run up the ramp to the spot where Nels Dagsen lay dead in a puddle.

The grid, which some people jokingly referred to as Norwegian hydraulics, was located in the North Harbor, just a block from downtown Petersburg. The grid consisted of several massive beams laid perpendicular to a huge retaining wall. If a skipper needed to repair a part of the boat that would normally be underwater, he ran the boat over to the retaining wall and waited for the tide to go out, leaving the exposed hull settled on the beams or "grid" and ready for the crew to paint or scrape. Or, in Marvin Brown's case, to pull the propeller.

Dan found the *Tlingit Pride* on the grid with the crew standing in a few inches of water staring at the stern. The tide was almost out. "Hey, where's the skipper?" Dan shouted as the rusty, barnacle-encrusted ladder to the beach twisted and lurched under his weight. The boat looked massive out of water. It was short but its hull was broad, beefy, and glossy white. A red and black Tlingit raven was painted on the bow. Its beak touched the tip of the boat and a spread wing embraced each side.

Dan watched Marvin, quick and agile for a man in his sixties, slog around the stern to a few yards away from where Dan was standing.

"You here about Nels?" Marvin asked.

"Yeah, but this doesn't look like the best time."

Marvin nodded toward the stern. "We're having problems with the prop."

"Trying to put on a new one or straighten out the old one?"

"Thought we'd put on a new one, but just about the time we settled on the grid, the jet overflew. The prop's on its way to Wrangell by now. We'll have to work with this one if we're getting out of here today." Marvin handed a canvas bag full of tools to one of his crewmen. "We got three, four hours max before the tide comes back in."

"Stop by the station when you get off the grid," Dan said as he headed back toward the ladder. The chief would carp all afternoon, but the chief didn't grow up around tides. He didn't understand that sometimes interviewing was pointless and this was one of those times. He wasn't going to learn anything from Marvin when Marvin had one eye on the tide. Besides, what were the chances that Marvin Brown was a murderer? Yvette was right; he wasn't acting like a man who's worried about a murder, he was acting like a man who's having problems with his prop. There was still that raven on the bow, though. How often do you have two Tlingit ravens cropping up in one murder investigation?

If Marvin only had a few hours before the tide was in, then the police department only had a few hours to find the gun. That was what they needed to focus on. He wondered who the chief would put in charge of the search. Dan wanted the job. That project was nice and concrete; Dan knew exactly how he'd do it, and it might keep him from having to deal with Lilly Dagsen. The chief didn't seem to be giving much thought to who did what, and if Dan asked to do the search, the request might just send the chief into another rant about old girlfriends. The Juneau specialist was stuck on the jet, so the footprints were on hold. The whole investigation was under water.

12:00 P

Dan worked through the case as he drove home. He couldn't ignore the fact that his childhood friend Lilly Dagsen could have killed her brother. She had the time, and the guts to do it. She had motive. Sure she'd been tender hearted when she was younger, but she'd been gutsier than him when it came to dares. She'd do anything without hesitation. And she was a different person now, that was obvious. What caused her to change like that? he thought. But even as the question was processing, his mind hopped on to the next concern—the lack of manpower.

They needed more help. The tide would be flooding soon, the Juneau guy was on his way to Wrangell, and the rain, or liquid sunshine as the locals called it, would be destroying every last bit of evidence on Stadsvold Trail. The investigation was hitting one road block after another, and Dan knew enough about small town murder cases to know people would be looking for any conceivable errors, real or otherwise. And the chief seemed to be primarily worried about the hook. They needed his help with the investigation but he was spending his time putting out political fires.

Dan's cell rang as he turned toward Papke's Landing. "Bad news, Buddy." It was Arne, the dispatcher. "The jet over-headed, so the Juneau guy is going to try to catch the ferry out of Wrangell tonight. If the jet doesn't make it into Wrangell, he'll wind up in Ketchikan and we'll have to wait 'til tomorrow to do prints."

"Dang, Arne, prints aren't going to last in this kind of weather."

"You'll figure something out."

Dan didn't have Arne's confidence, but he did have a plan. It included getting his oldest son, Jake, involved in the case. It wasn't necessarily a good idea; but under the circumstances, he couldn't think of an option.

Aside from its inconvenient location, Dan loved his home. He'd built most of it himself and knew every log on a first-name basis. His wife said log houses were dark and dusty, but to him the wood stove and honey-colored walls were relaxing. She'd hung frilly curtains in the kitchen, but he took them down the day he read her letter, and now the simple log rooms were warm and restful.

His oldest son Jake had been home from Iraq for a year now, and he enjoyed debriefing with the boy. Usually the discussion revolved around who had gotten drunk and done something stupid over the weekend. It was always interesting to hear Jake, who typically witnessed the event, give an objective version of the story.

Dan raised both his sons to work hard, and Jake had followed his father's counsel. A basketball star in high school, the way he handled the ball set him apart from other players. He wasn't known for accuracy, or height, or hands, he just played with his entire heart. When he ran out on the court, the team rallied and the crowd screamed. After every game he was surrounded by adoring middle schoolers wanting their program autographed. Since he'd returned from the Army, he'd been building a small log house on the lot adjacent to Dan's.

"Hey, big guy, got a minute?" Dan walked into the kitchen.

"Hear FC got broke into last night," Jake said with a smile.

The Fishing Co-op, or FC, a combination grocery, hardware, electronic, clothing, furniture store where one of Jake's many girlfriends worked, had been founded by Petersburg residents in 1920. It still used pretty much the same bookkeeping method as when it was first established: random crewmen, wives, or children could go to FC and charge things to the boat account—groceries, potting soil, oil skins, power drills, La-Z-Boy recliners, anything they needed. The store clerk kept a running tab for each boat, and at the end of every month, the skipper got the bill. The system, which was rarely abused, didn't require anything more than an honest face and the number of the boat account.

Dan wasn't surprised that Jake already knew about the robbery. He'd probably been waiting all morning to discuss the break in. "Everything we investigate solves itself for more than a year, and then we have two honest-to-goodness crimes in one night," Dan said. "The chief is bringing in a guy from Juneau to work the footprint angle, but the plane over-headed."

"I can do the tracks, Dad," Jake said. He and a friend had been avid trappers in high school, and a science teacher, a former Border Patrol officer, had taught them how to cast tracks. By the end of their junior year, the boys had flawless sets of wolf, bear, otter, deer, beaver, and moose tracks. They had made molds of any track they found on the island, including the footprints of a couple of girls who had come over to take saunas.

"I need to warn you, if one little thing gets botched, they'll call a mistrial and you'll be crab bait." Dan had been considering the idea since he heard the plane overhead. The case was his priority. But now that he was actively discussing the idea, he started worrying about his son.

"Come on. I've got the skills, and I can handle the pressure."

"The chief's already watching my every move; he's afraid I'm going to make a mistake and he'll wind up getting shit-canned for hiring me. You'd better be sure you want to take this on before I walk into his office and say, 'Hey Chief, Jake did prints of his girlfriends in high school, why don't we let him practice on the first murder investigation we've had in decades?'"

"Look, Dad—I can do these prints better than the guy from Juneau. Especially since it's still raining, and he won't get to them until tomorrow. Let's go in to talk to the chief."

"Okay, Son. Get ready for a wild ride."

1:00 P

Two problems motivated Dan on his return to the station: The foot-prints, Jake could handle if the chief let him, but the tide was a con-stant coil in the back of his mind. The Wrangell Narrows, with an average fifteen-foot tide, would engulf the search for the gun in a few hours. He usually admired the tide's relentless continuity, but today it was just another obstacle preventing him from catching a murderer—like the rain washing away the prints, and the fog keep-ing the Juneau investigator out of town.

As Dan walked into the police station, he found the chief staring at a red cookie tin centered on his desk, and he remembered another of the investigation's obstacles—the chief's sudden animosity. "Hey, Chief, how's the search for the gun going?"

"I haven't checked; Arne's on it."

Internal alarms sounded at the thought of the dispatcher in charge of something as vital as the search for a murder weapon. "Has he got things started? It's past slack water."

"I guess he's got things going; he went down there about half an hour ago." The chief had spent most of his life in Minnesota where water levels remained constant. He didn't grasp the time restraint the tide put on the case, and instead of focusing on the need to focus, he gave Dan a meandering update on their lack of progress.

Arne had rounded up a handful of men with metal detectors and headed to the harbor. The plane hadn't made it into Wrangell either, so the hotshot investigator landed in Ketchikan. The ferry was plugged full of five hundred high school students heading home from the Southeast Music Festival, and the Juneau guy would have to wait and take his chances on tomorrow's jet.

Sy spent the morning processing the Fishing Co-op fingerprints. A couple of findings stuck out because they didn't make any sense. First, FC hadn't actually been broken into. The back door was wide open when the clerk arrived; it was more like someone had broken out. The gun case and cash register were fine, but a box of shells might, or might not, have gone missing. And finally, the vinyl recliner, everyone's favorite seat in the break room, was wiped clean of all fingerprints.

"Now, that's interesting," Dan said.

"Interesting, but useless."

"I don't know, Chief. I think we should strip the vinyl off and send it to Anchorage. Get it tested for DNA."

"Remind me when you were put in charge of this case." Lines on the chief's forehead deepened.

Dan took a long breath. The beginning of a headache nudged the base of his skull. "So where's the hook?"

The chief jutted his jaw toward the red cookie tin on his desk where a smug Norwegian troll grinned at Dan from the lid. Dan gingerly opened the tin to find the hook nestled in a stack of paper towels that smelled of cardamom and sugar.

"A cookie tin? Kind of like a Norwegian safety deposit box," Dan said. On a good day, he could coax the chief out of an ugly mood with a Norwegian joke, but today's attempt went flat. "I thought I'd head down and give Arne a hand with that search. Make sure things are set up before the tide's in."

"If we found the FC gun, and it was the murder weapon, we could narrow our search down to the break-in. That would be huge." The chief leaned back and considered. "I still don't know what to do about those damn footprints, though."

"Listen, Chief. I'd like to turn Jake loose on the prints."

"Are you serious?" His voice rose as he shot upright. "That's what I'm trying to avoid."

"So what's your plan? Let them soak?"

"That's better than putting a kid in charge."

"Jake can handle this, and you know it. You're not worried about Jake, you're worried about the Norwegian Mafia. You think this case is about keeping the public happy, but it's not. It's about catching a murderer." The knot in his neck twisted one rotation tighter. "Maybe people will think Jake's a mistake, but sitting on our thumbs while those prints dissolve is a guaranteed, front page editorial waiting to happen."

The chief placed the lid back on the container as the bearded gnome grinned, happy to find himself in the midst of a confrontation. "I thought a small town in Alaska was the perfect place for a cop. No murders, no crime. Come to find out, a small town in Alaska has everything a big city has. But in the small town, you know everyone involved and you're working in a fish bowl." The chief wiped invisible crumbs off the tin with his hand and then added, "Okay. Tell Jake to come talk to me. I'll get him started on the prints."

"Good, and I'll check on Arne," Dan said.

"Hold on. What about this morning's interviews?"

"Can we talk about it later?"

"Just give me your take on Marvin Brown."

"I didn't have much of a chance to talk to Marvin."

"You're joking, right?" A storm settled on the chief's forehead. "He's our strongest suspect, and you haven't questioned him? What the hell have you been doing?"

"Look, Chief, we need to get a couple of things straight." Dan's calm face contrasted with angry eyes. "You hired me, you can fire me; that's your choice, and I don't question it for a second. But you don't get to treat me like a screw-up unless I screw up." He paused for emphasis and continued. "So fire me, or quit breathing down my neck. I've got a job to do."

"You don't understand how much rides on this case." The chief's response was close to a whine. "It's like the hook—no one paid attention when nothing was happening, but now that we've got a murder to investigate, we're everybody's business. And your history makes you the prime target."

Lots of people in the tiny fishing village acquired jobs in unorthodox ways, but Dan's hire caused a political squall. At the bar several years ago, a man close to twice Dan's size had made a comment about Sy's ethnicity. The guy correctly guessed that Sy was too even-tempered to respond. But he incorrectly guessed that Dan was too small to respond. Dan tamped several of the man's teeth down his throat, and someone called an ambulance. Normally no charges were pressed in a barroom brawl, especially when the guy who started the fight wound up in the puddle of blood. But there were so many witnesses that the police had to show some sign of interest; they charged Dan with disorderly conduct and sentenced him to 160 hours of community service—at the police station.

By the time his 160 hours ended, Dan had impressed the entire department, and they didn't want to lose him. He was smart, hard working, and trustworthy. He was painfully ethical. He got along well with the staff, and the chief liked having him around. Tongues wagged and fingers pointed as the chief nudged Dan up the law enforcement ladder. First as a dispatcher, then dog catcher, and, finally, police officer.

But the locals had a long collective memory, and that caused a problem. Sy could make a lot of mistakes and no one would mind. So could Arne and the Juneau guy. But if Dan screwed up, folks would blame the chief for hiring a hothead.

"Half the population's watching to see if we damage the hook, and the other half is watching to see if we bungle the investigation. The mafia is looking for an excuse to run me out of town," the chief said.

"I hate to break it to you, Chief, but the third half of the town's watching to see how you handle Lilly Dagsen, and you can't imagine what a hornet's nest that is going to turn into."

He stood and leaned on the chief's desk. "Chief, I'm sorry, but I don't have time for this. The tide's coming in and we're going to miss our opportunity to find that gun. I'm not going to sit around and wait for this investigation to fall apart. Shit-can me if you want, but I'm headed to the harbor. And while you sit there worrying about your image, you might want to spend a quick second worrying about how to get this investigation a little organized."

Well, things don't get much better than this, Dan thought as he jogged to the Middle Harbor. People were looking for a tiny mistake that they could twist into a colossal police department blunder. And he'd put Jake right in the middle of the maelstrom. His first thought was that Jake could do the job on the prints. His second thought was that Jake would make a good cop, and maybe the chief would recognize his son's potential if he saw the boy in action. But ultimately, he'd put Jake in the center of a dark, ugly cloud that could follow his son for years.

And then there was Arne. The dispatcher had a hard time answering the phone on a good day, much less handling something as crucial as a search for a murder weapon. Dan couldn't believe the chief had put him in charge of something that pivotal.

And finally there was the tide. It just kept coming in.

1:30 P

Dan watched Arne and his helpers, clustered on the beach in an odd assortment of scrufty, orange oilskins, wool jackets and rubber boots. The men stood, hands in pockets, kicking rocks and watching a hundred pound black lab cavort through the mud. A chain dragging from the dog's collar left undulating trails through soggy paw prints.

The tide spread insidious tentacles toward the beach, but Dan couldn't take his eyes off the dog running unchecked through the middle of a murder investigation. "Whose black lab is that?" he asked as he approached the group.

"Looks like Hal Rich's," a searcher said.

"Somebody call him a cab and send him out to Hal's place." The animal bully-ragged a long piece of bull kelp in protest.

"How's the search going?" Dan asked Arne.

"Ah, we just got started." Arne nodded toward a couple of men weaving along the beach swinging metal detectors.

"Okay, let's start by dividing the area into sectors. Call FC and have them send a stock boy down with a few rolls of flagging tape and a half-pickup of cinder blocks. Tell them we're looking for the gun, and we're trying to beat the tide. They'll hustle." He watched Arne start the call and then continued to the rest of the group, "You guys, divide the area from the Poor Man's Float, to the beach, to the North Harbor into about thirty sections. Then we can take each one, and cover every inch of it. If we don't find the gun in one, we'll move over to the next."

The group moved slowly until Dan pushed. "Come on, guys, we're racing the tide here." That was something they could all relate to. A couple of men shouted orders and the group plunged into action.

"Arne, call the dive shop and ask them for a list of divers. Get them down here as fast as you can. This whole place will be under water in no time. Ask them if they can bring a truck for filling tanks, too."

A man walked up carrying his metal detector. "I should have worn different boots." He rolled his eyes sheepishly and nodded toward his low-cut Xtra-tuffs.

"Don't worry about it, Stan. We need a tent that the divers can warm up in. Can you work on that?"

"Absolutely!"

In forty-five minutes, long pink streamers tied to cinder blocks outlined a football field-sized grid running parallel to the beach. A yellow, eight-man tent dominated the parking lot, and several divers in fins and neoprene, packed diving tanks toward the beach. The black lab had been wrestled into the back seat of a taxi, a rusted-out Plymouth that had transported more than one dirty dog in its day.

Dan watched the scrambling volunteers and wondered how many times these men had raced Mother Nature. Fighting the tide to get their skiff in or out of the water, or their gear on or off the boat, or their boat up or down the Narrows. And now, to find a killer. "You've got this under control, Arne," he said as he slapped the dispatcher on the back and jogged toward his truck.

His mind moved on to the Raven Hook. It fit in somehow. It had to. That was what he had to work on next. Not following up on Marvin Brown was going to get him in more trouble with the chief, but he was sure Marvin Brown wasn't the killer. He'd take the heat at their next debriefing, but right now he needed more information. The hook was key; it was just a matter of finding where it fit.

2:30 P

Dan headed a mile out the road to Severson's Subdivision where Sam Varga, Forest Service anthropologist, museum board member, and good hunting buddy, lived.

"You hear about Nels?" Dan asked when he arrived at the Vargas' square, single story home.

"Gee, no, Dan. What happened?" Smile lines crinkled the corners of Sam's eyes. He was so quiet and polite people thought he was Canadian. "I'm not a suspect, am I?"

"Yeah, this case has all the earmarks of an anthropological serial killer," Dan said, handing Sam a stack of photos. "Did you know we found Nels gripping one of those old halibut hooks?"

Dan thought a talk with the anthropologist would calm him, but close to twenty antique clocks ticked loudly in Varga's living room. Sam didn't notice, but Dan, already on edge, felt his nerves fraying.

"Yup, that's the Raven Hook, all right. Look at all those bite marks around the base; it caught a lot of fish in its day," Sam said, thumbing through the pictures. "It was perfectly preserved when Old Man Dagsen found it up Petersburg Creek. Luckily, he tossed it in a bucket of salt water to bring it back to town. These old artifacts disintegrate before your eyes once they hit air." The anthropologist studied the pictures and then added, "Shit, Dan, it looks like it's already falling apart."

Dan caught a quick glimpse of the chief's perspective on the case, and that insight caused a sudden wave of self-doubt. Maybe he'd been too hard on the guy. His boss's theory, that some people were more worried about the hook than the murder, rang true. Dan thought in terms of a murder investigation, but a lot of people, even this close friend, thought in terms of irreplaceable artifacts rather than bodies. "I gotta get out of here, Sam. Let's head to the museum."

The two men discussed the hook as they drove; they ignored the rain, the wind, and even the incoming tide as Sam answered one question after another about the hook. The more questions Dan asked, the more he appreciated the artifact. "So Old Dagsen found the hook at the mouth of Petersburg Creek, and it's a big deal because it was so well preserved, right?"

"It's a big deal because it's a big deal. There were thousands of those hooks at one point, but wood and cedar don't last. But the Raven Hook had the sense to settle in a perfect blend of mud, sand and gravel." Sam smiled the smile of a man who appreciates fine sediment. "And that perfect combination just happened to be located in groundwater with a high iron content." His face radiated the look of a happy anthropologist. "The sediment and ground water combined to keep bacteria from forming. No bacteria, no decay. And there we have it: a priceless, one of a kind, irreplaceable artifact. I'd rather lose my left hand than have that hook damaged."

Dan glanced up Hammer Slough as they passed, but the searchers weren't visible.

"Alaska didn't have anybody who knew how to deal with a find like that, so an archeologist from the Museum of Natural History came up. He put it in a chemical wash of polyethylene glycol for over a year before he dried it out to display in the museum. It was carbon-dated at close to two thousand years old."

"Jesus H., no wonder the town is in a snit. I guess the big question is how it got to Sing Lee Alley," Dan said.

"That's the stumper. Dropping something like that in your pocket and walking out of the museum would be mighty gutsy."

"But it's a raven. That's relevant, right?"

"I doubt it. The raven's a descent group for Tlingits, Haidas and Tsimpshians. But that won't tell you much. I'd say the guy who pinched the halibut hook didn't even know what he was grabbing, or he would have taken better care of it." Sam thought for a moment before continuing. "Something that old. We'll never see anything like it again. No one who understood would leave it in the rain overnight."

They continued exploring possibilities until they reached the Clausen Memorial Museum, a tiny, L-shaped, one story building adjacent to a weed trimmed, three-car parking lot. Between the parking lot and the entrance, a copper arrangement called *Fisk*, the

Norwegian word for fish, splashed water over a school of metal herring making the tiny fish flip and swim as if they were alive.

"When we were in elementary school, we used to come on class trips to look at the petrified dinosaur dropping," Dan laughed. "This little place has come a long way since then."

"It sure has," Sam said, as he inspected the oxidized copper sculpture. "I remember when they changed the label from *dinosaur dropping* to *coprolite*. It was a cultural advancement for all mankind."

The inside of the museum showcased the community's fishing heritage. A Fresnel lens from the Cape Decision Lighthouse beckoned from one corner of the main room. Visitors admired this lens for its French engineering that multiplied a few lumens of light into a brilliant beacon, but the locals' admiration was more practical. In the 1930s this sentinel had guided salmon- and herring-laden vessels through the Inside Passage. The lens had provided safety for loved ones, and it was revered for that reason.

The world's largest salmon, now stuffed and dusty, occupied another corner. The salmon hung from a fishing line held by the image of a cannery worker. Looking at the 125 pound salmon, it was hard to tell if the cannery worker was displaying the salmon or the salmon was displaying the cannery worker—they were about the same size. This fishing display was what Dan and Sam had come for. The card naming the Raven Hook and the piece's history sat in the center of the display, but nothing was left of the hook except its faint outline in dust. "I wonder how long it's been gone," Sam said.

"Not long. The spot where the hook sat isn't dusty yet." Dan laughed, "Dang. I'm starting to sound like CSI Miami."

"You're going to wish you were working for CSI Miami by the time this is over."

When Dan and Sam left the museum, they took the registration book with them. Marret Engvold, the docent, assured the men that everyone had signed it over the long weekend. It looked like the usual handful from Ballard and a small group from Japan were the primary visitors. One signature, the illegible scrawl of a man Marret referred to as "a nice looking blond young man" had *Iraq* listed for address.

"All the way from Iraq to Petersburg's Little Norway Festival. Someone was really hungry for lefse," Dan said as he studied the registry. The Little Norway Festival was a unique experience. Tourists came thousands of miles to watch the locals exhibit their four-day Viking persona. Modest, good natured girls named Caryn morphed into breast plated Valkyries named Carnage and rode around in the Viking Mobile kidnapping innocent tourists and encouraging them to drink beer and dance.

"Maybe he wanted to learn to *pols*," Sam said using the Norwegian word for folk dancing.

"Gives new meaning to the term poll dancing," Dan said.

Sam's information didn't help tie Marvin Brown to the case. If they considered the raven relevant, half the Native population was suspect. And the museum hadn't helped either. What was it they kept harping about in training? The first forty-eight hours—those were the magic moments. If you didn't get your murderer in the first forty-eight, your chances of finding him went down to twenty percent. And here they were, close to halfway to the forty-eight hour mark and not a thing to show for it. Evidence was dissolving around them, or getting buried in the tide, or sitting in the station because they couldn't get it out of town. The chief and Lilly Dagsen were sniping at him every time he made a suggestion, and now he'd even put Jake in the middle of the investigation.

Well, this is a category five shit storm, Dan thought as he headed toward the station.

3:30 P

Sunday was the last day of the Little Norway Festival and a few die-hards had set up booths on Main Street. Things were slow. Most self-appointed Norwegians just ventured out of the hotel to locate their preferred hangover remedy, but occasionally someone would stop for chicken adobo or the rosemalled platter they hadn't bought the day before. For the first time in his life, Dan ignored the Salvation Army fry bread on his way to Stadsvold Trail, where he found Jake crouched under a sophisticated confusion of tarps and lines shrouding the murder location. A handful of curious locals monitored Jake's progress as he drained and tidied sections, poured molds, and numbered and organized prints.

"Kind of like ravens on trash day." Jake grinned and nodded at the observers.

Watching his cautious, methodical son restored Dan's peace of mind. He was annoyed years ago when Jake spent so much time making molds for a high school science project—Dan thought his son should be spending more time on math. Now here he was, using his tracking skills, not his math, to help with a case.

4:00 P

Dan dropped the museum register off at the station and started the harrowing trek to Lilly's apartment. He needed to get her list of alibis. And he also needed to look her in the eyes when she answered his questions. He wanted to go over exactly what he was going to say, make sure he kept control of this interview. The last meeting had been a joke, and he wasn't going to let that happen again.

The Pastime Café seemed like the perfect place to collect his thoughts before talking to Lilly, but it wasn't. On a typical day the café's steady stream of regulars took "shifts" at the choice tables and bar stools. The seiners showed up around six thirty in the morning and stayed until seven thirty, when a group of power walkers arrived and chatted until the nine o'clock old timers settled in. A group of professionals on their ten o'clock coffee break left a set of dice in a cup on the windowsill and rolled every day to see who paid for coffee. Every December 7, one WWII vet camped out on the stool that he was sitting in when the radio announced the bombing of Pearl Harbor. For the most part, the floods and eddies at the Pastime were as regular as the tide. Today, though, one shift after another had stuck around. Loflotin' Johnny was still hugging a coffee cup at the counter, and the entire dining area was buzzing.

Dan nodded to Johnny and scanned the room for a seat. Each group claimed its own area—the seiners flanked Johnny at the counter, the old timers roosted at the back two tables—but as Dan looked for an empty spot, everyone wanted the inside scoop on the investigation and began shouting invitations to join them. Arms waved like flags in the rigging and the din rose to World Series proportions. Dan smiled and nodded, then turned around and walked back out of the Pastime, around the building, and up the steps to Lilly's apartment.

He simplified his plan: be relaxed, but professional. He could do that.

Dan tapped on the door and studied Lilly's welcome mat as he waited. The mat showed a rosy-cheeked Norwegian troll saying "*Velcommen.*" When he was a child, the school librarian told elementary students that trolls pulled children into muskeg ponds. It was a draconian method of child rearing, but children had sometimes drowned in these little ponds, and the mothers accepted the terrorism if it kept their children safe. Now, ironically, the chief stored the halibut hook in a cookie tin with a troll on the lid, and Lilly had a troll on her welcome mat. Trolls are just waiting to suck me into the muck, he thought as he knocked again.

Lilly opened the door and stared coolly at Dan for a moment before stepping aside to let him in. It was a passive gesture, but enough to destroy every bit of his already diminishing equilibrium.

The floor of Lilly's harvest gold kitchen creaked as Dan stepped in. "Hey, Lilly. Thought I might ask you a few more questions. Do you have a minute?"

"Oh, sure, I've always got time to talk to someone who thinks I murdered my brother."

Dan's nerves spiked, but he was determined to keep the interview as casual as possible. "Did you put together that list of people who could verify you were at the Fish-o-Rama?"

She walked to the old Frigidaire refrigerator and found the list behind a blue rosemalled magnet.

"Frigidaire," he said. I haven't seen one of those in years. Remember when your dad told us Frigidaire was the Norwegian goddess of love, and we believed him?"

"That joke is even less appropriate now than it was when we were kids," Lilly snapped.

Well, what the hell, he thought. She seems to think she's wearing her big girl panties, might as well start treating her like a big girl. "I need the clothes you were wearing last night, too. We'll test them for mud from Stadsvold Trail." He focused on her facial expression and added, "And blood and gunshot residue."

Her eyes widened, but she headed for the back room without comment. When she returned, she carried her mother's red and black Norwegian dress, a pair of black shoes, and a crisp, white blouse draped in plastic. Dan's stomach lurched at the sight of the dress.

"You wore your mom's dress to the dinner?"

"Of course."

"The blouse looks like it's brand new."

"I just washed and ironed it."

"Are you serious? You've washed the blouse since last night?"

"I served food for hours in that blouse. I washed it for church this morning." She set her jaw, "And then, you know what, Dan? I washed it again. So I could put it away until next year."

"And let me guess. You bleached it, didn't you?"

"You know what the water's like in this town. Of course I bleached it." Her hands tightened to fists as she spoke.

"Get a grip, Lilly, this isn't an argument about ice cream flavors, this is a murder investigation. Use your head."

"I'm sorry," she said, her voice syrupy, her cheeks pinking. "If I'd known I was a murder suspect, I would have worn a dirty blouse to church this morning."

"You're taking this too personally, Lil."

"Don't be silly, I can't be taking it personally – we don't have a personal relationship."

Dan's thoughts circled like the copper herring in the museum sculpture, flipping and splashing but not going anywhere. Lilly had washed her shirt, practically an admission of guilt. People don't stay up washing and bleaching clothes unless they have something to hide.

And that damn dress, floating out of the back room like a ghost navigating a murder investigation.

Grandma Dagsen brought that bunad back from Norway the summer before Lilly's mom died. The family had gathered in the Dagsen living room as Grandma Dagsen pulled one treasure after another out of her suitcase: a tiny blue enameled forget-me-not bracelet for Lilly, Norwegian sweaters for Nels and Old Dagsen. She saved the best for last, handing the final parcel to Lilly's mom. It was wrapped in layer after layer of shushing, red tissue paper. Lilly's mom untied the jute chord and the long, black skirt unfolded like a grand gesture.

Lilly loved it instantly, and her mom said she could wear it when she grew up.

The day of her mother's funeral, Lilly foundered, awash in an eleven-year-old's grief. She had grown up the moment her mother died. From her perspective, it was her role to wear the Norwegian dress, but the black wool skirt kept sliding off her tiny frame. She hung it from the red vest with a tangle of safety pins.

Old Dagsen was furious. You didn't wear an ill-fitting dress to a funeral. They argued for hours. He insisted she take it off, but Lilly refused. Dan felt sick remembering the confrontation, he'd been sure Old Dagsen was going to hit Lilly, but that lithe, blonde, seventy-pound girl won her argument with a sixty-year old bully. She wore her mother's bunad to the funeral. Lilly and her father's relationship changed after that. She had chipped away a tiny bit of his control.

Lilly started taking care of Nels and Old Dagsen, and Dan started taking care of Lilly. For the next several years, taking care of Lilly was his primary concern. And now after all this time, no matter how much she had changed, no matter how much she snapped at him, every cell of his body wanted to take care of her again.

It made no sense. He'd lost his objectivity. He had to stay away from her, that was all there was to it, but the chief was insistent. And the chief was right: he should be able to handle Lilly after all these years. What was wrong with him, anyway?

5:00 P

As he walked to the harbor, Dan inspected Lilly's neatly printed list of contacts:

> 9:00 to 4:00, Decorated w/ Nancy;
> 4:00 to 5:00, Set tables w/ Helmi;
> 5:00 to 6:00, Cooked w/ Kari;
> 6:00 to 9:00, Served w/ Helmi, Kari, Glorianne, Nancy;
> 9:00 to 9:30 Took break at Fisherman's Memorial w/ Nancy and Kari;
> 9:30 to 11:00 Put away tables and chairs w/ Nancy and Glorianne.

Nancy Goodman, a fifth grade teacher and Lilly's best friend, was the most consistent name on the list. Too bad they were such good friends. With the murder scene minutes away from the dinner, Lilly's alibi was what the police force called soft.

When Dan got to the harbor for the second time that day, it was transformed. The parking lot was cleared and a six-wheeled pickup hunkered next to the ramp leading down to the float. Several tents created a festive atmosphere heightened by a handful of men and women walking around in blue or black, full-body dive suits. One woman wore a bright yellow suit with a yin yang sign on the back—obviously catering to Little Norway's Buddhist marine life.

The harbor teemed with colors that evaporated and intensified. Long strands of hot pink plastic tape twisted and swayed like psychedelic bull kelp. The surface of the water broke with a splash and a goggled, alien-like diver shook his head and began a breaststroke toward the beach. A child helped him with his weight belt and then bowing under the heft of it, carried it with arms outstretched, like an offering, to the shore.

Dan found Arne at the top of the ramp, hands tucked into the bib of his oilskins for warmth. "We haven't found anything but a couple of nice hunting knives. And there's enough propellers down there, it doesn't seem like anyone should ever have to buy another one," Arne said.

"Nice job, Arne, you've really got things set up. How much territory have you covered?"

"From the ramp to about halfway over." Arne's gesture included the area from the Poor Man's Float, the finger at the end of the ramp, to the North Harbor where the larger fishing boats sojourned in rows of tidy slips.

Dan rested one foot on the railing and leaned forward, studying. "So think like a shooter. If you were running from the trail, where would you pitch the gun?"

"Well," he looked in the direction of the trail and then back to the railing. "Probably right along there somewhere." Arne waved a long, gnarled hand toward the cannery side of the ramp, the opposite end of their search grid.

"I'll bet you're right. Would you throw it hard or just drop it?"

"Oh, I'd throw it hard, alright."

"You think? Seems like you'd worry about someone behind you, maybe someone who heard the shot and came to check. So you'd just kinda flip it in with a plop, shielding it with your body."

Arne turned abruptly. "I'll be right back." Minutes later three divers ducked out of a tent carrying their tanks and walked toward the beach.

Dan and Arne leaned forward, arms on the top railing and one foot wedged on the bottom, while tussocks of fog settled around the cannery buildings and reduced Petersburg Mountain to a hulking shadow across the Narrows. A shout from the water fractured the rain's steady sibilation. The woman in the yellow dive suit waved a slim arm clutching a plastic bag over her head. "I found something!"

"We got it! I'll bet we got it!" Arne's face split into a grin. "Right where I told those divers to look."

"Good job, Arne." Dan slapped the dispatcher on the back as the two men headed toward the beach.

As preoccupied as Dan was with the case, he couldn't resist admiring the .44 magnum. Its six-inch barrel was stainless steel and the handle was black with a diamond texture that someone could easily grip in wet weather. A local hunter had stopped a charging bear by shooting its knee out with a .44 magnum, and the gun had been popular with the locals ever since. Dan usually thought the long barrel was sinister, but enveloped in a Ziploc bag and a handful of water, it looked benign. Like something you'd bring home from a pet shop and hope your parents would let you keep. It was hard to imagine it could have stopped a force like Nels Dagsen.

6:00 P

The chief's desk harbored ferry manifests, lists of jet passengers, museum and hotel registries: the accumulated debris of a murder investigation. Arne had called in the good news, and the chief looked relaxed when Dan handed him the plastic bag holding a wet Smith and Wesson. "Well, Doc Wood pulled a round out of Nels' chest. It looks like the shooter used a .44 caliber, alright," the chief said.

"And FC is missing a Smith and Wesson .44?" Dan asked.

"Yup. We'll wait for word from Anchorage, but looks like we've got our murder weapon. Here's my best bet: Marvin Brown snatches the Smith and Wesson from FC, walks down toward the Fish-o-Rama looking for Nels, finds him on the trail, shoots him, chucks the gun off the ramp, and goes to the Harbor Bar for a drink."

"I don't know, chief. That seems pretty random for a murder."

"Well, hell, what's your theory?"

"Has the museum registry helped?"

The chief and Sy had worked on out-of-towners, and accounted for most of the people in the museum registry. The Ballard tourists, all friends of Patti and Gloria's, gave each other alibis for the entire weekend. The Japanese tourists roomed at the Scandia House, stuck together at the Fish-o-Rama and didn't know Nels. The Japanese interview ended when one of the tourists asked the interpreter if there was someplace in town they could buy a whoopee cushion.

Three other couples signed the registry: one stayed at the Broom Hus B & B, one at the Valhalla B & B, and one at Johnny Valsdad's parents' house on First Street. They were all in town for the festival, didn't know Nels, and didn't want their weekend ruined by a murder investigation.

"Who else did Marret say was at the museum? What about that clean-cut guy from Iraq?" Dan thought he should be a priority.

"We can't figure where he was staying. I'll put a Muskeg Message out on the radio for anyone who had visitors, see if we find him." The chief continued with his own thoughts. "The tourists are matching the passenger lists for the jet just fine. We'll keep following up, but I doubt it was an outsider."

"I don't know, Chief. Sam Varga says locals wouldn't touch the hook because we respect it too much," Dan didn't like the chief's theory. He knew almost everyone in town and didn't want to think one of his friends or neighbors was a murderer.

"Well, he's an anthropologist. He can develop all the anthropology theories he wants. I'm a cop; I'm going to stick with cop theories and that means Marvin Brown is looking good." The chief's face reddened.

"Has anyone else talked to Marvin?"

"Sy's talking to him now, since you seemed to have such a hard time doing it." The chief focused all this attention on Dan. "You're the bottle neck in this investigation. When are you going to follow up on Lilly Dagsen's alibi?"

"Listen, Chief, someone else needs to deal with Lilly Dagsen; she's not even willing to communicate with me." Dan returned the chief's stare and braced for the storm.

"Aw, for crying in the night! How many years have you been out of high school, anyway? All we need from her is a halfway decent alibi and information about her brother. Deal with it."

7:00 P

"Come on in, Dan." Nancy Roundtree walked back toward the kitchen. "Luke and I are just sitting down to dinner." She put a plate and silverware on a denim placemat and offered him a chair.

Nancy and her husband Luke lived in Scow Bay, a little less than halfway between downtown and Dan's place. Nancy had been teaching in Seattle when she met Luke, a former Ketchikan boy, and the couple decided to settle in Southeast.

It didn't take Nancy long to master the local cuisine, and Dan polished off a serious serving of Middleton Island Turkey—halibut, sour cream, cheese, and cream of mushroom soup —with rice and salad as he watched an Alaskan ferry on its way north. Like most of the people with homes on the Wrangell Narrows, Luke and Nancy lived on the second floor for the best view, and the dark blue, four hundred foot ferry, the *Malispina,* looked close enough to come through their living room window. He could see tourists with binoculars trying to get their first glimpse of town. "Isn't it annoying to have people staring at you through their binoculars? It looks like a couple of folks are discussing what we're having for dinner."

"I always want to take a piss off the deck, but I'm afraid Nancy will report me," Luke said. His tall, lanky frame was all elbows and knees in the small dining room chair.

"He *knows* I'll report him," Nancy said as she started making coffee.

Luke's gaunt face crinkled into a full out grin. He was clearly proud of his hardheaded wife. But when the dinner turned toward dessert, the conversation turned toward Lilly and the Fish-o-Rama. "Lilly was at the dinner the whole time. It was crazy hectic. All the Sons of Norway members are stretched pretty thin during the festival, and Lilly and I were running like wild women." Nancy carried a stack of dishes to the kitchen. "All I know is every time I hollered about something, Lilly hollered back."

"She said you went out to the Fishermen's Memorial for a while. What time was that?"

"I don't have any idea," Nancy said.

"It might help Lilly if you could narrow down the time."

"We'd already bussed the dinner dishes and taken a break before we started on the dessert plates. It was after the Viking Mobile," Nancy said. "Around eight thirty. We sat out in the gazebo for a few minutes."

"Was anybody with you?"

"Kari Johnson for the first few minutes. Maybe we were out there longer than fifteen minutes. We listened to a bunch of tourists singing 'Who Left the Halibut on the Poop Deck' for a while. They'd had more than one too many beers."

"Maybe you caught the Coast Guard choir rehearsal," Dan said.

"That makes sense." Luke couldn't help commenting. "They're all a bunch of choir boys." Local men harbored a special dislike for the Coast Guard, or the Ankle-deep Navy, as some men called them. More than one Petersburg man had lost a sweetheart to a fast-talking Coast Guard ensign. But more importantly, the local life-long fishermen resented getting boarded and pushed around on their own boats by eighteen or twenty year-old boys with relatively little nautical experience. A forty-year old man doesn't like getting questioned by a nineteen year old who calls the fo'c'sle a forecastle.

"The Fishing Co-op guys said Lilly was in and out of the FC all day," Dan said.

"During the day, sure. Every time we needed something—extension cord, duct tape—Lilly went and got it. And around five we all went home to change. But once the dinner started, Lilly stuck around. I remember she said something about Nels when he showed up. You know how he acts in a crowd. Like he's running for office. Talking too loud, shaking everybody's hand. It drove Lilly crazy."

"And that was around eight thirty?"

"Maybe closer to nine. I don't know."

As Dan thanked Nancy for dinner he considered just how random her timeline was. He understood why eyewitnesses mucked up cases. She was adamant about Lilly's alibi—so adamant that it made him wonder. But there was one aspect of police work that the visit clarified. Don't get too friendly with the people you're interrogating. It was impossible to question someone who had just fed you a huge plate of Middleton Island turkey.

9:00 P

"So how are things going?" Jake asked. The wood stove idled, and the small living room was warm. A gun safe and racks of fishing poles replaced the knickknacks Dan's wife Emily left behind, and braided wool area rugs covered an unfinished plywood floor.

Dan started a detailed debriefing. When he mentioned Marvin Brown, his son interjected a disbelieving, "No way!" but for the most part, Jake sat and absorbed his father's account of the investigation.

Jake didn't interrupt until Dan mentioned his waspish treatment from Lilly. "What's up with you and Lilly, anyway?"

"Nothing's up."

"Something's up, Dad. You two never talk, don't even look at each other, but you must know her from high school."

"That doesn't mean we have to be best friends twenty years later."

"Yeah, but Lilly always singled out me and Rocky. It seems like you and Mom would have been friendly to her, but I never saw either one of you so much as talk to her."

"Lilly and I hung out in high school. That's all."

"So you 'hung out' in high school, and by that I'm assuming you dated, and then you can't even talk to her years later? That's harsh," Jake said.

"She went to Norway as an exchange student for her senior year and I went in the Army."

"Okay, so let me rephrase things. She went to Norway and you enlisted and now you don't talk to each other? Still seeming harsh."

"There were issues."

"What? Like Lilly stole your firstborn child?"

Dan went to the kitchen and returned with a beer. "When your mom first got here, some old gossip mentioned Lilly and me. You know, something along the lines of 'I always thought Dan and Lilly would get married,' and your mom came unglued."

"Mom didn't even know Lilly, but she was jealous of her?"

"When we first got here, Lilly was a huge part of this town. She was at the center of everything—Sons of Norway, school events, Pioneers. But your mom always felt like an outsider."

"Yeah, but Mom would have to expect that. I mean she didn't grow up here."

"But she had this idea that she was second choice. We fought about it all the time. The first fight—it took weeks before she settled down. Then a few months later we had to duke it out all over again. When you came along she calmed down and things were good. Then they went south again; same thing: I should have married Lilly and everyone would be happy. All my friends liked Lilly more. *I* obviously liked Lilly more. When she got pregnant with Rocky, I thought things would get better, but they got worse. Then she had two little boys, and I was out fishing all the time, and that left her alone to imagine all kinds of things. I'd come in from fishing, dirty, exhausted, hadn't slept in sixty hours, and the second I set foot in the door, she'd start the same old fight."

"Was Mom's letter right when she said you never cared about her?" Jake said.

A pair of ravens carried on a discussion of their own outside the living room window. "By the time she took off, she was right; I didn't care about her anymore. But I was still trying to keep things going for you and Rocky. I never dreamed we could muck things up as bad as we did."

"And it was all because she was jealous of Lilly?"

"Everything helped. We stopped hanging around with old friends because they were always telling stories about Lilly and me. 'Remember when Dan and Lilly jumped off the oil dock on New Year's Eve?' or 'Remember the year Dan and Lilly both won the free throw contests at the Southeast basketball tourney?' So that was that. We had to stop hanging around with friends I'd known my whole life."

"That's rough."

"And for some reason Lilly took a special interest in you and Rocky. She was always going to your games. She didn't have kids of her own, so I guess she thought she had rights to you guys. Lilly would sit a few rows in front of us and stand up and cheer when they announced you or Rocky. Your mom would radiate heat."

"But in the beginning you loved Mom?" Jake asked.

"Your mother was so goddamn insecure. It could take your breath away. I could never understand how someone so smart and beautiful and funny could be so friggin' insecure. When we got married, I thought she'd become more self-confident, but just the opposite happened."

"Well, why did you and Lilly break up in the first place?"

"Jesus H., Jake. Forget it, okay?"

"Just this one last question."

"I'm going to bed," Dan said, as he walked his empty beer bottle to the kitchen.

"So how much of this does Rocky know?"

"I don't have any idea what Rocky knows. He's always been pretty insightful, but he doesn't talk. You, on the other hand ...."

Rocky had also enlisted right out of high school, but while Jake was willing to risk his life in combat, Rocky wanted an employable skill, so he signed up for the Sidewinders instead of the Screaming Eagles. He was spending his time in Afghanistan trying to keep sand out of heavy equipment engines. Jake was honest, dedicated and idealistic while Rocky was honest, dedicated and practical. Both boys, though, had always wondered about the deferential treatment they got from Lilly Dagsen.

Dan listened to Jake and Rocky Skyping late into the night as his mind hopped from one thought to another. First, he was incapable of doing a second rate job, so he would worry this case until he had it solved. And second, he was faithful to a fault. It had gotten him in trouble in the military and now it was clouding his judgment in the investigation.

Lilly was the best friend Dan ever had. In spite of their past, and in spite of the snarky treatment he was getting from her now, he still felt like he owed her an allegiance. He knew each detail of her childhood; she confided everything to him. As a police officer, he should tell the chief those confidences because they were relevant to the case. But as a friend he couldn't break her trust, no matter how she was treating him now, and no matter how many years ago their friendship ended. Telling the chief about her past would reopen wounds that Lilly spent most of her life trying to forget.

Thoughts churned through his mind for hours. He kept seeing the sweet, vulnerable Lilly of elementary school, and the hard-headed Lilly who ran the household after her mother died. He had been crushed when she cheated on him; she'd been so much a part of his life that he didn't know how to function without her. He didn't dream one person could have so much of an impact on someone, and he didn't feel whole for years after she left him.

Lilly's dad died in the summer after their junior year. Nels was already out of high school and living on the boat, so the question was what to do with Lilly. She solved the problem herself by going to Norway as an exchange student. She was pretty when she left—gray eyed and pink cheeked—but she was breathtaking when she returned; her face and body had filled out; all her angles had softened to curves. She flourished in that year away from her father and brother.

The night Lilly got back from Norway was the night she and Dan had seriously talked marriage. They sat on the lowered tailgate of Dan's truck and stared at the limitless dark blue sky. Lilly wore Grandma Dagsen's Norwegian sweater and faded jeans. A cool breeze tossed Lilly's hair and she had to keep pushing a lock of curls off her forehead as they huddled, arms wrapped around each other, and named stars. Lilly said one group of stars looked like a ring, and Dan said it would be their engagement ring until he bought her one of her own. Some women would have angled for the real thing, but Lilly said, "It's perfect. I'll always know where it is." It seemed so silly now.

Then Dan had gone into the Army. His dad wanted him to get out of Petersburg for a while. He'd said, "If you want to spend your life here, that's fine. But first you need to get out and see the options."

Things started out okay. Dan didn't get a letter every day, but he didn't mind. Lilly's letters were funny, not boring like the ones his friends got that were just a list of everything someone had done: "I took a bath, I shaved my legs…." Still, a few guys teased him about how he didn't get letters as often as they did. They said Lilly spent all her time with someone else, and it was just a matter of time until Dan found out about it.

And the Army kept telling him she wouldn't wait; the drill sergeant screamed about infidelities every time someone lagged, and even the cadences warned him:

> Ain't no use in going back,
> Jody's stole your Cadillac.
> Ain't no use in going home,
> Jody's stole your girl and gone.

At first he knew Lilly was different, but then he began to wonder.

Then his buddies' letters started dwindling. They'd come twice a week instead of every day. Then they'd get short little scrawled things once a week, and finally none at all. A couple of his friends got Dear John letters but most of them heard the news second hand. They quit teasing Dan about his weekly letters, and watched wistfully when he went off to his bunk to savor Lilly's every word.

And right when he started thinking that it was going to work, right when he got his confidence back because Lilly was still sending letters when no one else was, she'd skipped a couple of letters. Just like what happened with everyone else. She got a job and didn't have time to write. And she started talking about C.J. Schwartz, the guy who helped her get her job. He was so funny and such a nice guy and so great to work with.

Dan had seen it often enough, he knew what was coming.

When he got a letter from Yvette telling him Lilly was screwing around with C.J. Schwartz, he wasn't even surprised. Her next letter arrived a few days later, but he didn't even bother reading it. He couldn't stand the thought of seeing it in words. It took him a while to pull himself together, but he'd never looked back. He'd taken care of Lilly Dagsen for years, and the minute things got inconvenient, she ditched him.

Dan was tired of thinking about Lilly Dagsen. He needed sleep. Or at least to think about the case instead of Lilly. But after years of walling her up in a corner of his mind, she seeped back into his thoughts. He fumbled in the crawl space behind his bed and found the last letter he had ever read from Lilly:

> Hey Dan – Sorry my letters are running late, but I've got good news. I got a job at the bank. I don't think the manager wanted to hire me, but C.J. Schwartz talked him into it. He's been working there for a few months now and they love him. He's really fun to work with, too.
>
> But the problem was that I didn't have anything to wear. I've spent the last week altering a few of my mom's skirts into plain, straight skirts that I can wear to the bank. You should see me, I look so professional.
>
> I've been missing you. I keep going up to your mom's to talk to her. To go through your old scrapbooks and stuff. She loves having me there so we can talk about you, but then when your dad comes home we have to change the subject because he gets pretty disgusted with us.
>
> Your mom told me she thinks things will work out fine for us. I know it will too. Here's my theory, and you can correct me if I'm wrong: we were the only two

people in our class with gray eyes, right? And your right eye has that one little green freckle in it, and my left eye has one little blue freckle in it, so we practically match….

And a week later she was screwing around on him.

He didn't owe Lilly Dagsen a thing. All he had to do was keep his head down and get this damn investigation resolved. Life would get back to normal, and he could get back to ignoring Lilly Dagsen like he had for more than twenty years.

MONDAY, MAY 19

*This is an island, … and the talk can twist round and round
till there's a whirlpool in the washtub.*

- Sena Jeter Naslund

7:00 A

Dan hunched over his coffee listening to rain hit the metal roof. Their forty-eight-hour window was squeaking closed, and nothing was jelling. At least Jake had poured the footprints. And the gun. They had the gun. But still, they were a long way from any solution, and the clock was ticking.

"Hey Dad, I wanted to catch you before you left."

Dan's long night was punctuated by the sound of his two sons Skyping until late. Something important must have gotten Jake up so early this morning.

"You sound serious."

"Yeah, kind of ruin-your-day serious. Joey Olsen told Rocky the latest rumor, and I thought you should hear about it. Sounds like Nels Dagsen listed the *Norge* for sale in next Thursday's *Island Trader*."

"I'll be go to hell. Just the boat?"

"The boat, permits and a whole butt-ton of halibut IFQs. And here's the catch: the word is he was selling his fishing operation to get enough money together to start a fish farm in Metlakatla."

"Shit, no wonder somebody killed him."

"That's not all, Dad. People are saying that Lilly wasn't too happy about it."

"Well, that's a no-brainer."

"Yeah, but they're saying that's why she killed him."

"Just like that? Lilly's the killer?"

"Think about it. If Nels sold the boat and reinvested the money in a fish farm, Lilly was one step closer to never seeing her share of the inheritance. It gave her a pretty good reason to kill Nels."

"Aw, nuts!" Dan said as he squeezed past Jake and into the bathroom. This news was a game changer. A soft alibi like the one Nancy provided last night wasn't enough. "Where was Rocky when you talked to him?"

"Still in Afghanistan," Jake shouted over the shower.

"Aw, nuts!"

Dan negotiated Big Red onto the highway behind a derelict flatbed stacked with piles of swaying crab pots. The rear fender bobbed with each pothole, taunting Dan with its "Friends Don't Let Friends Eat Farmed Fish" bumper sticker.

His mind on Nels Dagsen's fish farming scam, he took the Beachcomber curve at fifty. The idea was brilliant from a business perspective. As a fish farmer, Nels wouldn't be nearly as regulated as a fisherman who answered to the Fish and Game, OSHA and the Coast Guard. Nels could hire a small crew and spend the rest of his life virtually regulation-free while he put the local fishing fleet out of business. One thing you could say about Nels Dagsen, he never missed a self-serving opportunity. Of course, it looked like this particular self-serving opportunity might have gotten him killed.

Lilly should have told him about the fish farm. The whole time he'd been questioning her, she'd had a crucial piece of information she didn't bother mentioning. Did she actually think he wouldn't find out? Little Miss Dagsen might know a whole lot more about this murder than I gave her credit for, he thought as he raced up her steps two at a time and pounded on her door.

"We need to get some things straightened out," he said as she opened the door. "Why didn't you tell me Nels was selling out to start a fish farm in Metlakatla?" But his anger dissolved when he noticed her eyes, puffy and rimmed with dark circles.

"That's crazy. Nels hated fish farming as much as anybody." Her tremulous voice slowed Dan's momentum even further. It was true, the Petersburg fishermen universally despised fish farming: the price fishers received for wild salmon plummeted when farmed fish began glutting the market, but that hadn't stopped Nels. "He has the whole show listed in Thursday's *Island Trader*," Dan said as he studied her blotchy face.

"Well, that's the story of my life." Lilly threw up her hands and plunked down on the couch. "Right when I start thinking he wasn't an asshole, he proves me wrong. Even when he's dead! I was actually starting to grieve, and then I hear something like this, and I hate him all over again."

She chewed a fingernail in distraction. "Last night I started looking through old photo albums. That was a big mistake. There was this one picture of Nels and me in our Underoos—remember, that underwear designed like superheroes? Nels was Superman and I was Wonder Woman. We were both flexing our muscles and grinning at the camera; our little arms looked like chicken wings." Her voice broke.

"I know he was a bastard, but he was my brother." She wiped her eyes on her faded blue Petersburg for the halibut T-shirt. "I thought even if I never had kids of my own, I'd have nieces and nephews someday." With this final thought, she brought her knees up to her chest and began sobbing.

"Okay, Lilly, take it easy." He sat next to her on the couch, fighting the temptation to put his arm around her. He couldn't come in physical contact with a suspect. Especially Lilly Dagsen. As quickly as he'd sat down, Dan jumped back up and headed for the kitchen. Shit, I'm hopping around like a fart in a skillet, he thought as he escaped. "You need something to eat, and then we need to get a few things figured out," he shouted. He took eggs out of the Frigidaire, and put them on the burned and pockmarked counter. Lilly had arranged her kitchen just like her mother's, and Dan found the garlic salt, bread and glasses right where he expected them.

He placed the pan on the burner with one hand and set the temperature with the other. Lilly followed him into the kitchen and smiled when he started cutting holes in the center of buttered bread. He was making eggs-in-a-hole, the first dish they had learned in eighth grade home ec.

Dan laughed outright as he put mint-green melamine plates on the table. "You've still got your mom's old dishes?"

"Mom and I ate Shredded Wheat for years to get those free dishes. They're the only family I have left." Her laugh was strained, almost hysterical.

She sat and the kitchen table and continued. "Nels always ranted about farmed fish. Too much waste. Too many chemicals. Mushy flesh. 'Would you care for a side of sea lice with your salmon?' Then he turns around and sells the *Norge* so he can open a fish farm of his own? It's unbelievable. And in Metlakatla? Why Metlakatla?"

"Met's the only Indian reservation in the state. It would eliminate a lot of government interference. But, you're missing an important point, Lil. You're looking at things from your own perspective, and you need to look at them from an investigator's perspective. This fish farming scam gives you an immediate, multimillion-dollar motive to kill your brother. You need a concrete alibi and you don't have it."

"Uff da." Lilly looked like she'd been sucker punched.

"It-sha," Dan replied. "How much are the boat and all the permits worth? A few million? So Nels took millions of your dollars to speculate on the most hated industry in the state. People have killed for a lot less than that."

"But I didn't know a thing about it! I wouldn't have killed him if I did know, but he didn't have the right to sell our property. Especially for something as destructive as a fish farm." Her cheeks reddened in frustration. "He ruined my whole life. Everything. If anybody understands that, you do. And now he's dead, and he's still just as toxic as he was when he was alive. I'll wind up in prison because he decided to start a fish farm with my inheritance." Tears rolled down her cheeks as she grasped her brother's final injustice.

They both had their arms resting on the wooden table. Its glossy, white surface was uneven from years of painting and repainting. They were so close, Dan thought he could feel heat radiating from Lilly's hands. He fought an urge to reach toward her by folding his hands on his lap. Shit, now I look like a librarian, he thought, and then dropped his arms to his side. He couldn't remember the last time he'd felt this uncomfortable. It took him a second to re-focus. "Okay, Lil. It's time for you to lose the attitude and start helping with the investigation. I need some straight answers. First I want to understand why you never just took Nels to court and got this straightened out."

"Take a look around, Dan. Are you really that clueless?" Lilly gestured toward her shabby apartment. "I buy one pair of shoes every two years. I eat the school lunches, for crying out loud. How am I supposed to afford a lawyer?"

"But don't you think a lawyer would take the case and get paid once it was settled?"

"And go up against Nels Dagsen? Are you serious?"

As Lilly continued her explanation—the lack of legal precedence, her own fear of Nels, the local reaction—one unstated point emerged: If she permanently severed her ties with her brother, she permanently severed her ties with the only family she had, and that final cut would be too much for Lilly to bear.

Dan was uncomfortable realizing exactly how much family ties had meant to someone who was raised in such a dysfunctional situation. "Well, there's someone out there who hated Nels enough to kill him. We need to figure out who," he said in an abrupt attempt to change the subject.

"That's all I've thought about. I can't imagine."

Over breakfast they discussed the possibility of a crewmember killing Nels. A few of Nels' crewmembers had talked to Lilly about short crew shares. The problem was that Nels knew just how far he could push things without making it worth the crew's money to hire a lawyer. He also made sure they didn't have access to solid documentation like fish tickets. But Nels' crew was upset with him at the end of just about every season.

"Why'd they even keep fishing for him?"

"Nels knew where to fish. He had all of Dad's old fishing logs, and he came up with a few spots on his own. He hired guys away from other skippers and then pumped them for information." She shoved her plate away untouched. "If a boat was consistently on fish, he'd hire one of the crewmen, get him drunk or promise him a bonus or tell him his old skipper was badmouthing him, and find out how to fish the new spot. Then he'd add it to his charts." Lilly shook her head as she remembered her brother's duplicity. "The thing is, it worked. Nels' crewmen could comfortably support a family on their crew shares."

"What about the old *Norge*? There were always rumors he sank it for the insurance money. Could there be anything from that far back?"

"We never talked about it, but I'm sure he sank the old *Norge*. I think Earl Sanderson was in on it somehow. They did a lot of talking right around the time it happened."

"Blackmail might fit in there somewhere. I'll talk to Earl. Who else might want him gone?" Dan asked.

"Well, Trina Davis." Trina Davis was the one female deckhand Nels had ever hired. They had an affair when she was a senior in high school. Nels hadn't married her, but that made her feel even more venomous toward her ex-skipper. "Trina's dad said he was going to kill Nels, but I think he would have done it by now if he was going to—it's been twenty years."

Dan explored every possibility with Lilly. He even asked if Low Floatin' Johnny could have a motive for murder, but Lilly only laughed at the idea, and he had to agree: Lofloatin' seemed a little too laid back to bother killing someone.

"What about the fish farming angle. Who else might kill Nels because of a fish farm?"

"A fisherman might fill the back of his truck with crab bait, but no one would kill him." She considered for a moment and then added, "What about an environmentalist?"

"An environmentalist?"

"Yeah, they like fish farms even less than the fishermen do. And a militant environmentalists might even have the guts to do something about it."

"Okay, I'll start chasing down some of these folks. You get a lawyer."

And that was it. All the equanimity that had settled between the two dissipated in a fog of misunderstanding. "Get a lawyer? That's it? No discussion, no exchange. You make a royal decree, and I'm supposed to drop everything and get a lawyer? You know, Dan, you're a police officer, that's all. You don't get to tell me what to do. Just because we have one civil conversation every twenty years, doesn't give you the right to step in and take control of my life."

Shit-oh-dear, what was that all about? Dan thought as he thumped down the rickety stairs. One minute she's all 'Oh, poor me in my Underoos' and the next she's screeching about lawyers. That's it. I'm going to stick to the job. Cross one suspect off the list and move on to the next. And if Lilly Dagsen is the only one left, well hell, I'll go after her.

She's the one with the motive; I should be taking her more seriously anyway. If someone took my money and invested it in something as sleazy as a fish farm, I'd consider murder. And the farther her money got from the old *Norge*, the less likely she was to ever get her hands on it. Her right to half the permits was already murky, and once the money was invested in a fish farm, Lilly might never see any of it. Twenty years was a long time to wait for an inheritance that was already hers. Maybe she had finally decided to do something about her self-serving brother and his expanding empire. Who could blame her?

Lilly was right about the environmentalists, though. If word got out that Nels was preparing to start a fish farm, the environmentalists were just as militant as the fishermen. Dan's dad had a logger friend lose a leg when his chainsaw hit a spike driven into a tree. People said that was from an environmentalist, but they had never known for sure. He'd take a look at the tree huggers, but that wasn't going to stop a lot of people from suspecting Lilly. The way she was acting, maybe they were right.

8:30 A

In the short drive to the police station, Dan passed the detritus of the four-day festival. Lane-wide Norwegian and American flags slumped over Main Street, straining rain onto the cars below. Rows of beer cans lined benches and gutters. Paper plates and cups tumbled in the wind. A Velcro shoe and a child's plastic Viking helmet kept each other company on the lid of a trash bin—the poor man's lost and found. The town looked more than a little hung over.

The reduction plant added its own special flavor to the cheerless streets. The local fish processors thought that the day after the Little Norway Festival was the perfect day to decompose herring carcasses and turn them into fertilizer. Recycling the waste was a federal mandate, but what the feds didn't realize, and probably wouldn't care about anyway, was that the stench permeated the town for days. It wasn't an odor or a scent, it was a full-blown, eye-watering stench. People didn't like to go out when the reduction plant was running: their skin and nostrils and even the inside of their mouths were coated with a fishy residue that clung to the town like barnacles to a hull.

Dan breathed through his mouth, trying to avoid the odor; taking one oily gulp of air, he held his breath and raced into the station. "Hey, Britta," he nodded at the weekday dispatcher who was checking her hair for split ends as he passed.

"You need to sign in," she shouted and then followed Dan down the hall to the chief's office. "How am I supposed to keep track of the officers when they won't sign in or out?" she said to the chief.

"Well, when you saw me, you could figure I was in —," Dan said.

The chief interrupted. "Britta, we're running at full tilt right now. Let's wait until things settle down a bit to initiate your protocol."

"Things sure go a whole lot easier around here when Arne's at the desk," Dan said after the dispatcher left.

"It doesn't hurt to have one person going by the book. But right now, we've got other things to discuss." He had talked with the state's transportation director about getting the manifest for Saturday night's ferry. A maze of paperwork and red tape initiated after 9/11 was resolved when the chief reminded the director that they had brought in a 220 pound halibut together on a fishing trip several years earlier. The director happily talked fishing and checked the manifest himself.

"Britta, will you make another pot of coffee?" the chief shouted down the hall. The two men went over the ferry manifest as Britta dumped fresh water into the reservoir. Both turned and watched when water slapped the floor, and the pot slammed the burner.

"The only people who got on the ferry Saturday night were the Fuglvogs. They were taking their van to Costco to stock up for the fishing season," the chief said. "So, it doesn't look like our murderer left town on the ferry."

"You know, Chief, I think we should check who got off and on the ferry in Wrangell, too." Dan was relieved to notice the chief was in a better mood, but then he remembered he had thought the same thing about Lilly before she exploded.

"Okay. I'll get Britta going on that. Anchorage gave us an esti-mated time of death between seven and ten. Since several witnesses say Nels was at the Fish-o-Rama between eight and eight thirty, we've already got a more accurate time frame than they could give us. I think it's safe to say eight to nine thirty."

"I bet we can narrow that time down a little further if we keep questioning people at the dinner," Dan said. "But I've got another little morsel that should shake up the investigation: According to Rocky, our buddy Nels Dagsen was just about to *carpe his diem*."

When the chief heard that the Dagsens' fishing operation would be listed in Thursday's *Island Trader*, he yelled down the hall, "Hey Britta, get Harry Baker on the line. Call him at home if he's not in his office."

"I'm working on all the paperwork that Arne didn't get done yes-terday," Britta answered on the intercom.

"Harry Baker, Britta," the chief repeated.

"It's a beautiful idea," Dan said. "He could market farmed fish as Alaskan salmon."

"You got to hand it to Nels, he was smart," the chief said as Britta announced Harry Baker on the line. "Hey Harry! Yup, Yup, Yeah, that's right," he said brusquely.

Dan was amused by the situation: the broker was pleased to get a call from the chief and wanted to chat it up a little, while the chief just needed a quick answer and an end to the conversation. "Yup, well I guess not. Hey, Harry..." the chief continued. "Harry," he tried again, and then finally, "Harry! I got an important question. I heard Nels Dagsen had the *Norge* and some permits up for sale...." After a brief pause he added, "How much you figure they'd sell for?" and then, "You know who he was working with in Metlakatla?" He cradled the phone and turned to Dan. "Well, I guess sometimes we get our best leads from Afghanistan. Rocky got that one right. Nels had listed somewhere between five and six million dollars worth of boat, gear, permits and IFQs, and told Harry to keep it quiet until Thursday. He said he had something he needed to do before then."

"I'm sure it was something intended to benefit all of mankind."

10:00 A

The rain had upgraded from the usual drizzle to an honest to goodness downpour. The spruce and hemlock looked almost black, and a powdery gray mist caressed the mountains across the Narrows. Dan turned his truck up Excel Street and headed to Trina Davis's house on South Third.

This was the same route he and Lilly took the day of her mom's death, and the memory came back in high definition. It was the week before fifth grade. They were riding their bikes to Knudsen & Holtan's to get school supplies.

The two of them saw an ambulance turning up Excel, and Lilly yelled, "Come on, Danny," and raced up the hill ahead of him. He could see the muddy brown stripe that her bicycle tire splattered up the back of her lavender hooded sweatshirt. Lilly's thin legs made her feet look huge in new back-to-school sneakers. She pedaled hard—standing and leaning the bike to the right as she pushed down with one foot, and then to the left as she pushed down with the other.

Dan remembered every detail. Mrs. Shanks's Chihuahua yapping at them as they sped past. The huge puddle in front of the Patrick's driveway rooster tailing when they rode through. The silvery white flowers cascading over Mrs. Fryer's concrete retaining wall. They were so intent on going fast that they almost rear-ended the ambulance before Dan realized it had stopped at Lilly's house. Two men were running in as Lilly's dad held the door open.

Lilly slid off her bike so lithely that it kept going, rolling into the spindly rhododendron by the front steps. Old Dagsen grabbed her with both arms as she ran past him, first yelling "Mom" and then "Mommy," growing younger as the realization pummeled her ten-year-old mind. She allowed her father to hold her until Dan's mom arrived and led her away.

As they drove off, he saw Lilly's dad standing, hands in pockets, talking to a policeman on the porch. Lilly's bike lay in the bushes, tires akimbo, the skeleton of a lost childhood. Her mom's death was listed as a suicide, but there was no note. A lot of people still thought Old Man Dagsen killed his young wife.

But there was a tiny pocketful of people who knew the details of the suicide, and they knew that Lilly had more than one reason to hate her brother.

Dan wove his way through the weeds to Trina Davis's dark green rubber trashcan, picking up soggy pizza boxes as he went. He tossed the trash in the can and snapped the bungee cords across the scratched and dented metal lid. He considered the fact that bear-proof cans didn't really seem to be much of a deterrent as he knocked on Trina's flimsy storm door.

"Hey Dan, I wondered if I was going to be part of the action. Sorry the place is such a mess, my son had some friends over." As Trina spoke, a couple of hung-over teens shuffled up the steep, narrow, Norwegian stairs. Dan caught a whiff of stale beer, either from the boys or the crumpled cans littering the room. Overflowing ashtrays, and Chinese take-out seeped onto thread-bare furniture, and Trina didn't seem to have fared much better than her living room. An orange and magenta flowered caftan draped her once petite body. Her face was still pretty, but her brows had been plucked to short, thin arcs of surprise, and her complexion was sallow. "Sit down." She cleared a spot.

"I heard you worked for Nels when you were in high school, Trina."

"Huh – that's not a pretty story. It started after an eleventh grade volleyball game. He came over and told me I really impressed him with how hard I played, and he was thinking about hiring a new crewman, and had I ever fished. Well, I was on top of the world—I couldn't believe it." She smiled as she remembered. "He was twenty-eight and already a highliner. Even my mom pushed the relationship." Trina shook her head. "As soon as school got out, I started working on gear for him. Too dumb and too in love to expect a paycheck. By the time seine season started we were foolin' around. I slept in the captain's quarters with him, and the rest of the crew stayed in the fo'c'sle. At the end of the season I assumed I'd be moving into his place." She punctuated the memory with a harsh laugh. "He made it real clear he thought different."

Dan heard muffled sounds in the stairwell and Trina shouted, "Junior, this is none of your god damn business," then continued with her story. She couldn't go home when the whole town knew she'd spent the summer sleeping with Nels. Her dad was drinking and she was afraid of the beating he'd give her. She'd begged Nels, and he finally let her move in for a few weeks, but about a month after school started, she came home to a new set of locks and everything she owned on the front porch. Nels had gone to Palm Springs to play golf.

Trina thought she could stay on the boat, but she found it locked. She tried to talk the harbormaster into letting her stay in the harbormaster shack for the night, but that was against city policy. Finally, the harbormaster gave her money for a room at the Tides Inn, and the next day the hotel hired her as a maid. She dropped out of school and never went home again.

"A couple a months later I caught him heading down to the boat with two of the crewmen. I lit into him big time, and he just stood there with that nasty smirk on his face. Finally he said, 'I tell you guys, it took a lot more than penicillin to get me cleaned up after that little piece of ass,' and they all laughed and walked off.

"I'd worked with those two crewmen all summer. I did way more than my share, so they wouldn't resent having a woman on the boat. I piled web every set, and then when we were running I'd go to the galley and bake cookies, homemade bread, fried chicken." She shook her head as she remembered. "I actually thought they liked me, or at least respected me. But they were just as happy to ditch me as Nels was." She fanned herself with a grease stained take-out menu before continuing. "I hated the guy enough to kill him, but I could never get my shit together to do it."

Another creak at the top of the stairs prompted a second outburst. "Back off, Junior. I swear to god I'll come up there and knock you ass-over-teakettle!"

"So where were you Saturday night, Trina?"

"Me and Ole Hanson and Tommy J. were here partying. Junior and a couple a friends were here, too. They'll vouch for me."

"What about your dad?"

"What about my dad? Shit, Dan, he's been in long-term care for six years now. Man, he gives those poor nurses a run for their money, but there's no way he could handle a murder. Besides, he doesn't remember much of anything. I doubt if he even remembers who Nels Dagsen is, much less the fact that he ruined his daughter's life."

11:00 A

Dan headed up Haugen Drive past the old, lime green Temsco helicopter hangar, the boxy city maintenance sheds and swampy muskeg patches. He noticed that the two stunted muskeg trees he and a friend had used to build a giant potato slingshot were gone. It was probably for the best. They had broken a picture window over a block away and had to work half the summer to pay for the damage.

Cars were parked two and three deep at the airport. Since the jet hadn't gotten in on Sunday, all the festival visitors were rebooked on the morning flight and mobbing the one-room terminal.

When Dan saw arriving passengers walking across the tarmac, he wandered into the terminal thinking about his wife Emily and her goodbye letter that listed all her reasons for leaving. Most of them were nonsense, but he could relate to the one that said she didn't want to live someplace where she had to walk across the tarmac to get off the jet. That was an accurate assessment of the town's size. Dan grew up walking across the tarmac when he got off the jet, and it never bothered him, but he wished it didn't remind him of his failed marriage every time he did it.

He wove between the meandering lines of people going through security and groups of people saying goodbye to visitors, and finally spotted a short, wiry man wearing a JPD fleece vest and a facial expression somewhere between a smile and a grimace. Dan made eye contact and offered his hand. "Dan Fields. Thanks for coming down to help us out."

"Nigel Eckles," the officer returned the handshake with a bone-crushing grip. "So you're Fields, the guy that got arrested and then wound up on the force? They got a funny way of hiring folks in Petersburg." His graying comb-over did little to hide the freckles on his scalp.

"Do people call you Nigel?"

"People call me Officer Eckles."

The silent drive back to the station gave Dan time to wonder about short men and their tendency toward bone-crushing handshakes.

12:00 P

The chief had coffee ready when the two arrived. A large plate of sandwiches sat on his desk. Smaller piles of folders and training manuals were stacked on the floor.

Eckles was more congenial in the chief's presence, but Dan attributed part of the Juneau officer's composure to the number of sandwiches he put away. Folding half a sandwich into a thick quarter, he dispatched it in three bites and quickly grabbed another.

I wonder if he has to unhinge his jaw to do that? Dan thought as he watched.

"Okay, Sy, now that the Juneau investigator is here, how about you give us the Native angle on this halibut hook," the chief said.

"There isn't a Native angle, Chief." Sy's discussion was more personal than Sam Varga's had been. He didn't call the Ravens and Eagles *moieties*, he called them *sides* and explained that everything in the Tlingit culture, including these sides, were intended to maintain balance. If something happened to one group, the other group took care of them. If a Raven died, the Eagle side made all the funeral arrangements, supported the grieving family, did anything they could to help.

"So look at Lilly Dagsen right now," Sy said. "She's just lost her only relative and she has to make all the funeral plans, try to get everybody into town, figure out how to feed everybody afterward. In the Tlingit culture, she would spend this time grieving while the other side took care of things for her. And took care of her, too," he added.

He paused, and when no one commented, he continued. "Okay, so Marvin Brown's boat has a raven on the bow. You Weegians think that ties him to the case," he said, "but there are a whole lot of people who have the right to use the raven as part of their identity—half of all the Tlingits, Haidas and Tsimshians in Southeast Alaska, for starters. The hook itself is relevant to the investigation, but the raven on the hook doesn't tell you a thing. I mean, I'm a Raven, and if I murder someone, I'm not going to leave behind a raven calling card."

"Am I hearing this right? You got a hook from the victim with a raven on it, and you got a suspect with a raven on the bow of his boat, and you think the two aren't connected?" Nigel asked.

"Well, that's what I'm saying; I don't know exactly what you're hearing," Sy said.

"I've been worrying about this hook for long enough. I think it's time to ship it off to the State Museum so we can focus on other things," the chief said.

"Juuuust a minute now," Eckles said, "I want to take a look at this hook. And then we'll need to send it to Anchorage for DNA testing."

Dan expected the chief to baulk, or at least explain the value of the hook, but he deferred to Eckles.

When the discussion got around to Jake's molds, Eckles seemed uninterested, but as they discussed other aspects of the case, he began twisting every piece of evidence until it pointed at Lilly.

"So did anyone think to get the clothes she wore at the dinner?" Eckles asked.

"Yeah, I've got her Norwegian dress and shoes bagged in the back room," Dan said.

"Let's Gold Streak those to Anchorage with the hook. I don't want you guys messing with important evidence," Eckles said. The chief nodded in agreement. "Has anyone brought her in for questioning?"

"We've talked to her," the chief said. "But she just lost her brother, and she's not really in great shape right now."

"Are you kidding? The best time for breaking down a murderer is when they're still riled about the crime. It's time to take off the gloves." He smiled as he chewed.

"Okay, Arne and Nigel. You two can bring Lilly here for questioning," the chief said.

Dan watched Eckles grab one more sandwich as he walked out. "So, Chief, when you said he was a wolverine, I didn't take you literally."

"We need someone who's objective, and this guy fits the bill. Now we've got some extra help, let's roll with it," the chief said.

"Okay, Chief, we'll keep you posted." Sy left the office and then waited for Dan to follow. "Just keep your head down and let the guy do his job so we can get him out of here, Dan."

2:00 P

Dan considered Eckles as he drove to the airport to meet Meera, one of Nels' many former wives. Sy was right, they needed to let the guy do his job, but it looked like the Juneau investigator had tunnel vision with Lilly Dagsen at the end of the tunnel. Dan had considered Lilly as a possible suspect, but Eckles was turning the case into a witch-hunt. He'd barely been in town for an hour, and he was already ignoring any information that didn't implicate Lilly, and what was worse, the chief was going along with it. Sy's warning to "keep his head down" was fine, but he wasn't going to sit back and let Eckles indiscriminately stockpile evidence against Lilly. Maybe the chief thought this guy knew what he was doing, but no matter how good he was, he wasn't good enough to drop into a case and decide who was guilty before he knew all the facts.

He was surprised to find Eckles hadn't located his favorite suspect when he saw Lilly's old Subaru at the airport. I'm disappointed in ya', Nigel. You're not at the top of your game, he thought, heading into the terminal.

Dan knew how to read a crowd, and the number of turning heads and disapproving glances as Lilly walked his way was not a good sign. It looked like Yvette was right: people were aligning themselves against Lilly. "Shit, Lilly. Half the people in here are watching every move you make," he said.

"I know. People who gave me a big hug yesterday are treating me like a leper today." Her voice was tight with frustration. "I don't understand what changed."

"They want to see you acting like the grieving sister."

"That Juneau officer just showed up at school looking for me." Her voice rose an octave. "My brother just died; I'm organizing a memorial service. So does he go to my apartment to find me? No, he goes to school and leaves a message with the principal that I'm supposed to go down to the police station for questioning about the murder of my brother. He might as well have driven through town with a loud speaker announcing me as a murder suspect."

"This guy is a real rat bastard, Lilly."

"I don't have anything to hide. I'll go toe-to-toe with him if that's what he wants, but I just can't stand everyone staring at me. If people have a problem, tell me what it is and give me a chance to explain. Don't just keep looking at me like I've just sprouted an extra head or something."

Dan took a moment to watch the jet approach from Fredrick Sound. As people in the terminal turned to see it land, he looked beyond Lilly to a family standing behind her. The parents and two sons were staring at her with a look that hovered between hate and hostility. For some reason the town's sentiments had flipped in less than a day. People hadn't even needed Nigel Eckles to start suspecting Lilly. Something had happened.

Dan didn't remember much about Meera Dagsen, Lilly's most recent sister-in-law, but he recognized her immediately. She wasn't more than five-two in her three-inch platform shoes. Shimmering black hair, one side held back with a clip, fell down to her tiny waist. As she spied Lilly in the crush, her face radiated a glow that made Dan smile. That guy knew how to pick his women, he thought.

As the women hugged and talked —Lilly all peaches and cream, and Meera all flashing jewel tones—Dan focused on other passengers. Departing travelers, mostly locals headed out for business or medical, were going through security on one side of the terminal. Arriving travelers were beginning to cluster around the baggage chute. They were easily identifiable as well. But one woman—tall, slim, and blonde—stuck out from the rest. Dan watched her as she stood to one side of the terminal and stared at Meera and Lilly. He wondered if Nels' death had brought her to town, but before the idea had even jelled, Dan heard an exclamation from Lilly: "Oh, my God! Anya?"

"Yah, hello, Lilly. I see you have friend." The blonde inspected Meera with interest.

"This is Meera, Nels' last wife."

Meera's shy smile charmed Dan, but the moment shattered when Anya said, "No, I didn't divorce Nels. I am his last wife."

Dang, Nels, Dan thought as he headed back to town. In the average lifetime, a guy might antagonize one woman into considering murder, but you managed to leave behind a whole flock of women who wanted you gone. And enough money to keep them sparring for years.

Either of the wives had a motive for murder. Anya and Nels had never divorced, so Anya had a strong case for inheriting. Meera didn't know she and Nels weren't legally married, so she at least thought she was in line for his money. It was interesting how quickly the two women made it back to town. They both must have thought they were on the money train.

All the staring and cold shoulders at the airport was unnerving, but now that there were three people with ties to the money, Eckles would have to lighten up on Lilly. And the fact that Nels had married one woman without bothering to divorce the other would remind everyone what a bastard he truly was. Things should ease up a little, Dan thought. But then, as quickly as the calm settled, an anxious apprehension crept back into his thoughts.

Why was he on Lilly's side, anyway? She had screwed around on him years ago, she screeched at him every time he tried to interview her, she may have withheld information about the fish farm, but as soon as Eckles decided she was guilty, Dan jumped to her defense. It's not that it's Lilly Dagsen, he assured himself as he drove, I'd be protecting anyone that Eckles had in his cross-hairs.

3:00 P

Dan approached the old Sons of Norway Hall with a certain amount of reverence. The barn-like building had been designed and built by locals in 1912 and was the oldest Sons of Norway in Alaska. The slats of the old wooden floor creaked a welcome as he entered the huge room where he had played basketball, sat on Santa's lap, and stuffed himself with lutefisk as a child.

His son Jake looked up as he entered. "Hey, Dad." He smiled and gestured toward three strips of molds about twenty-feet long, by five-feet wide. Jake had created an exact, reverse-replica of the crime scene on the scarred wooden floor of the old basketball court.

Dan admired the molds for several minutes and then started telling Jake about Nigel Eckle's arrival. "He's figuring Lilly for a slam dunk, so there's no reason to mess with anybody else."

"Well, I haven't met him, but my money's on Lilly. She can handle a guy named Nigel. Anyway, while you and Nigel bonded, I had time to take a look at these molds." As Jake explained the prints, the details of the project became obvious. About eighty percent or more were Xtra-tufs, a reddish-brown, rubber boot worn year-round by a majority of the population. Even in Juneau, the capital city, legislators of both sexes sported the "Alaskan tennis shoes" with their power suits. The theme for the last governor's inaugural ball had been "Tuxes and Xtra-tufs." It wasn't surprising that the rubber boot prints dominated Jake's molds.

Jake also pointed out a handful of generic sport shoes – Adidas made herringbone prints, Pumas made concentric circles, and Nikes made zigzags. Nothing seemed out of the ordinary except for one set of honeycomb prints. When Jake excitedly steered Dan toward the much smaller section of the Fishing Co-op molds, Dan couldn't see the correlation.

"Look at this one corner," Jake said. "It's about a half inch of the same pattern. It's probably not going to solve the case, but I bet the same person who wore those shoes down Stadsvold Trail wore them into FC at some point Saturday."

"Any idea what kind they are?"

"No, but I think I'll go down to Lee's and talk to Heidi or Cynthia. They're always up on that kind of stuff."

Dan walked back to the station, his mind on Lilly. The arrival of the two wives was to her advantage, but Nigel Eckles had already decided she was guilty. He wouldn't bother wasting time on anyone else. And Lilly really was the obvious suspect. Her brother destroyed everything of meaning in her life. Just the fact that she was a suspect at all proved his unfair treatment of her. If Nels hadn't been so self-serving, Lilly wouldn't even have a motive for murdering him. And he was going to keep right on plaguing her. Lilly would go through hours of grueling interrogation with Nigel Eckles—question after question about Nels and their childhood. Eckles would dredge up every morsel of her dysfunctional family and keep hammering her with the crippling memories. It was a miracle that Lilly had survived the Dagsen household and still managed to live a normal life, but now Eckles would bombard her with each horrible memory until Lilly said anything to be left alone.

Every police officer knew about false confessions. Totally uninvolved suspects admitted to crimes for a moment's peace or an hour's sleep. How long would it take Lilly to crumple when Eckles started asking her questions about her past? About Nels and her mother? About Old Man Dagsen's abuse? She was already worn down by Nels' death and all the work she had put in at the festival. No one has enough self-control to last indefinitely.

The more he thought about Lilly, the more sense the Tlingit moieties made. She was juggling two wives, an aggressive police officer, the death of her brother, and a gale of small-town speculation without any help. She needed a Raven or an Eagle to get her through, and she didn't have anyone.

And even if she didn't fall apart during the interrogation—even if she was never found guilty of Nels' murder—she would go through a lifetime of ostracism unless Dan found the guilty person. Look at how many people still thought her dad was a murderer. Someone would always keep the suspicion fresh. He had to find Nels' murderer, or people would consider Lilly a suspect until long after she was dead and buried.

Weegians are tough, he said to himself, but not that tough.

When he entered the station, it was no longer inviting; the florescent lights were a little more garish, and the linoleum was a little more scuffed and gray. The tawdry look distracted him for a moment. People coming to pay a ticket or to visit their friend or relative must feel like this. Hostility crouched in the corners.

To emphasize Dan's alienation, Britta greeted him with rancor. "That Juneau investigator is really making Lilly Dagsen squirm," she said with satisfaction. Short and thin, everything about Britta was pointy: her nose, her chin, her brows. She watched Dan pause outside the interrogation room where Nigel Eckles was questioning Lilly. "It's just a matter of time before she crumples," Britta said with a smile. Even her teeth were pointed.

The lighting, Britta, everything about the station was unsettling, but Dan's stomach twisted when he entered the chief's office and saw Sy and the chief exchange an uneasy glance.

"We need to talk," the chief said, handing a special edition of the *Petersburg Journal* to Dan.

Local Woman Implicated In Brother's Murder
Petersburg resident and elementary special education aide Lilly Dagsen (44) will have a difficult time proving her innocence in the recent murder of her brother, seiner and long-liner, Nels Dagsen (47).

All police investigations start with a search for the person who has three things: means, motive, and opportunity, and Lilly Dagsen has more than met those three criteria.

First Miss Dagsen had means. That is to say, she had the ability to commit the crime. Nels Dagsen was shot with a handgun that was stolen from the Fishing Co-op, and Miss Dagsen had access to that handgun on Saturday (the day of the murder).

The strongest of the criteria is Miss Dagsen's motive. Her brother has been running their family fishing outfit since the death of their father in 1983. He took a virtually valueless fishing operation and built it into one of the largest legacies of the fishing fleet. According to Harry Baker, the Dagsen fishing operation is worth an estimated $7,000,000.

The final of Dagsen's three criteria is opportunity, and as the *Journal* has discovered, she had ample opportunity to shoot her brother. As a matter of fact, we have found two witnesses who are willing to testify that they saw Lilly Dagsen running from Stadsvold Trail (the location of the murder) towards the Sons of Norway Fish-o-Rama Dinner at 9:00 p.m. Saturday night (the approximate time of the murder).

Besides filling the three basic requirements of means, motive and opportunity, Miss Dagsen had another reason to murder her brother. Again according to Harry Baker, Nels Dagsen had listed his entire fishing operation in Thursday's *Island Trader* with the intentions of re-investing the capital in an independent business.

Not surprisingly, Miss Dagsen has not returned our calls.

"This explains why everyone at the airport was staring at Lilly," Dan said. "I'll head over to the *Urinal* office to get the names of the witnesses."

"No, Dan, I think that's exactly what you won't do." The chief handed Dan another page of the *Journal*. This one contained an editorial:

Our Town Deserves Justice

One of the main reasons the people of Petersburg love our little town is because it is a safe haven from the rampant crime that occurs down south. Now that this rampant crime has come to our own haven, we expect the police department to do the job they have been grossly overpaid to do, and apprehend Nels Dagsen's murderer so we can get on with our lives.

We all know who that murderer is, and we expect an arrest; however, we also expect that arrest to stick. We have seen too many murderers go free on technicalities. A police officer doesn't Mirandize a suspect, or a lab confuses DNA samples and a known murderer goes free.

We don't want those kinds of problems to muddle our investigation, and so we appreciate the help of Juneau Police Department specialist, Officer Nigel Eckles. However, a sound arrest also requires that any person or persons that lack objectivity must withdraw from the case to ensure justice is done.

It has been brought to our attention that Officer Dan Fields should do just that. Officer Fields had a relationship with suspect Lilly Dagsen for an undetermined period of time, and a friend of Emily Fields, Dan Fields' former wife, informed the *Journal* that this relationship between Lilly Dagsen and Dan Fields was the cause of their divorce.

Concerned residents have seen Officer Fields coming and going from Lilly Dagsen's apartment at all times of the day and night, inappropriate behavior for a police officer under any circumstances, but especially unfit considering the current investigation.

We would like to remind readers that the *Journal* was opposed to Fields' promotion from dispatcher to officer, and now our concern has been justified. People that don't have the self-control to avoid common barroom brawls should not be police officers. And people who are intimately involved with murder suspects should not be investigating the relevant murder. This seems obvious to us and it should be obvious to Officer Fields. Petersburg citizens deserve a clean, un-appealed investigation and trial, and we will not get them unless biased persons such as Officer Fields are removed from the investigation.

"That's bullshit."

"I think this is one of the few times in his career the editor got things right," the chief said. "You're not objective when it comes to a long-term friendship like the one you had with Lilly, and, just as important, people *think* you're not objective."

"Yesterday I was trying to avoid Lilly and you were pissed about that. Now you've changed your mind because a newspaper editor who doesn't know if he should shit or go blind has decided to tell you how to run your department?"

"It's not just the newspaper. I've had some calls today. If we don't find the murderer, everyone is going to say it's because you were protecting Lilly. That'll be the public perception, and in the long run in a town this size, public perception is all that matters."

"I'm supposed to just sit back and let that little sawed-off marmot run this case?"

"You're still on the case, but stay in the background. You don't have a thing to do with Lilly until this investigation is over. You don't talk to her for any reason. You don't even say a casual 'howdy' when you pass her on the street. You especially don't 'come and go from her apartment at all hours of the day and night,'" the chief quoted the editorial.

"I can't believe you're bending over."

"Dammit, this is for Lilly's own protection! Any contact you have is detrimental."

Like most unpopular people, Eckles had an uncanny way of appearing when least welcomed. He strode into the office, turned a chair backward, and straddled it as if the gesture would somehow compensate for his lack of stature. "Boy, it doesn't take long for that woman to show her mean side," he said, ignoring the obvious tension.

"Okay, where do we stand?" The chief sounded overly chipper. "Dan, did Nels' wife come in on the jet?"

"Two of Nels' wives came in on the jet, and they both claim they're still married to him."

"Aw, Jesus, Mary, and Joseph," the chief leaned back and ran his fingers through his hair.

"You've got to hand it to Nels, it takes a real special touch to mess up as many lives as he has." Dan couldn't help but be a little pleased with the chief's reaction. "What about Wrangell? Has anything panned out from that direction?"

"We've got their PD following up on a couple of unknowns who have been in and out of there, but nothing concrete," the chief said.

"I'm not terribly interested in that," Nigel said. "But I am interested in Lilly Dagsen. Me and Britta were just conversating, and she says the whole town thinks Lilly's dad murdered her mother. Her dad's a murderer, she's a murderer. The apple don't fall far from the tree. It shouldn't take long to break her down."

Dan looked to the chief for an objection, but when none came, he pushed back his chair and stood. "I'm going to take a look around Nels' place."

"I'll come along," Sy said, following his friend out.

Dan ranted as the two men headed out to Nels Dagsen's ostentatious house in the muskeg. "Eckles will antagonize Lilly into saying something stupid."

"Nah, you need to give her more credit. She's smarter than you think. A whole lot smarter than Nigel Eckles," Sy said. "But what is the story with her mom's death? Her dad was a suspect?"

"Their family was so screwed up. Lilly's dad treated her mom worse than crab bait. He's smack her around for the craziest reasons—having the wrong thing for dinner or cutting the grass too long or too short. Trimming the shrubs or not trimming the shrubs. And he always hit her where the bruise wouldn't show. It was that calculated and controlled.

"But I think the mental abuse was worse than the physical abuse. Finally, her mom couldn't take it anymore and committed suicide." Dan turned up the hill at the ferry terminal. "They never found a note, though, so some people thought Old Dagsen must have killed her."

"Are you one of those people?"

"No, it was suicide. But it was especially bad for Lilly because her mom didn't leave a note. Didn't say goodbye. And now Eckles will use every horrible memory of her mom's suicide to get to Lilly." Dan pulled into Nels' driveway before he added, "Most of the time Lilly's pretty level headed, but when she gets angry she gets irrational."

"Hmmm, I know someone else who has that problem," Sy said. "And while we're on the subject, what happened between you and Lilly, anyway?"

Sy listened patiently to Dan's story of abandonment and then shook his head. "I wonder if your perspective is just a smidgen off center. My wife says you dumped her."

"Well who are you going to believe, me or Rita? I was there."

"I've seen the way your mind works. I think I'm going to stick with Rita's story on this one," Sy said as he stepped out of the truck. "Man, look at the size of that wood pile." The two men stared enviously at the tidy woodpile stacked the length and height of Nels' garage.

"Well, you know what Coach Olsen used to say: there are two kinds of men—the kind that hug trees and the kind that chop them down. I guess we know which kind Nels was," Sy said.

"Huh, Miss Evens used to say there are two kinds of men—the kind that like Best Foods and the kind that like Miracle Whip, and I have no idea where Nels stands on that one."

"Was she the home ec. teacher?"

"No, she was the typing teacher, but she knew a lot about sandwich spreads."

5:00 P

"This would have changed Lilly's life," Dan said, gazing out the huge picture window. He had a clear view of the distant mountains and an expanse of muskeg dotted with irregular ponds. A great blue heron crouched like a vulture in one of the hemlock trees at the edge of the clearing.

Dan and Sy stood in Nels Dagsen's second floor living room. The icy white walls, red carpeting and shiny black leather furniture made the room shiver with energy. Glass end tables and display shelves held basketball trophies, and one wall displayed mounted deer, moose, and caribou heads. A yellowed polar bear rug lay in front of the couch. An old oak desk holding an antique black and gold Royal typewriter sat incongruously against a wall covered with sport and fishing pictures of Nels.

The two men were looking at a letter that Sy had found wedged in the desk's long, narrow pigeonhole. It gave both the case, and Dan's nerves, an unexpected twist.

They had started the search with Nels' three-car garage. The walls were lined with tidy cabinets and the concrete floor was covered with dark blue rubber tiles. "This garage is cleaner than my whole house," Dan said.

"This car is bigger than my whole house." Sy opened the door on the black Cadillac Escalade and looked in the glove compartment. He held up a "Friends Don't Let Friends Eat Farmed Fish" bumper sticker and grinned.

"Maybe Nels didn't have any friends and that's why he could start a fish farm," Dan said. As Sy continued checking the passenger side, Dan reached under the driver's seat and pulled out a Smith and Wesson .44. "Well, we must be making progress: we went from no murder weapons to two murder weapons in less than a day."

"Think that .44 Arne found isn't the real weapon?"

"Yesterday I wanted to find a handgun so bad I couldn't stand it. Today, we're tripping over them." Dan smelled the barrel and dropped it in a plastic bag.

Nels' exercise room, between the garage and the staircase, contained a treadmill, an elliptical trainer and a Bowflex home gym, all facing a solid wall of mirrors. Two bedrooms with a common bathroom, complete with a sunken tub, finished off the bottom floor.

"Man, this is just the basement. There's no way the upstairs is going to top this," Sy said as the two men headed up.

"I bet Nels found a way," Dan responded. They weren't disappointed when they walked into the master bedroom. Its entire ceiling was covered with mirrors.

"I couldn't sleep under something like that," Sy said.

"Yeah, I'd wet myself every time I woke up and saw some ugly, unshaven guy on the ceiling staring down at me."

When each man grabbed a corner of the mattress and tipped it to one side, a magazine fell out.

"Oh, Nels, we found your porn stash," Sy said.

"Ah, to be more specific, we found your gay porn stash. What the hell was that doing there? No way Nels was gay." Dan bagged the magazine and they continued on to the game room where they found another huge television, an Xbox game console, a pool table and another wet bar, but nothing of interest.

That was when they headed for the living area, and Sy found the letter from Lilly's mother. The letter that Dan couldn't stop reading and re-reading.

"Dearest Lilly-Bug," it began. "I hope I can explain." More than thirty years after Lilly's mother committed suicide, Dan and Sy had found the missing suicide note.

"That note was all anybody talked about," Dan told Sy. "The cops ruled it a suicide, but it was pretty unusual for a woman to shoot herself. And it was even more unusual for a woman with a family not to leave an explanation. They really wanted that note to prove it wasn't a murder."

"Old Man Dagsen must have found it. Why didn't he just show the police in the first place?" Sy asked.

"He probably didn't want people asking questions about Nels and why he was mentioned in the note. Dagsen was heartless about everything except Nels. He would have protected his son no matter what." He looked at the yellowed paper and Lilly's mother's spidery writing:

> I hope I can explain. I was seventeen and pregnant with Nels when we got married. Your father was thirty-two. I was so stupid that I thought he was attracted to my maturity. And he had a boat and a house – it seemed glamorous – an Alaskan fisherman. I was going to be the perfect housewife and mother. I'd cook and clean all day in our perfect house, and our life would be perfect.
>
> I don't know what I did wrong. As soon as I started looking pregnant, your father lost interest. I thought once Nels was born, he'd fall back in love with me, but he never showed me even the tiniest hint of love or respect or kindness again.
>
> Grandma Dagsen looked out for me. The day she died was the worst day of my life. I knew I'd lost the only protection I had. Do you remember how I couldn't stop crying? I was afraid things with your dad would get worse and worse, and they did.
>
> I want you to understand. You have to understand. I love you more than anything in the world, but I can't take any more. I can't live with an abusive husband and an abusive son."

Dan skimmed the next several pages and then reread the last page, a disorganized ramble:

> I love you so much, I'm so sorry - I hope you can forgive me, Lilly Bug. You're strong, I know you'll be all right, but I can't go on like this. I love you. You're the only thing that has brought any happiness into my life, the only thing. I love you. I'm so sorry. I love you.

"This is going to crush Lilly," Dan said. "And it's going to make Eckles' plan that much easier. He'll spring this letter on her and then start wheedling away at what Nels did to cause her mother's suicide." Dan rubbed the back of his neck, where a knot was forming as the two men spoke. "He's going to chew her up like one of those sandwiches he was inhaling for lunch."

"You know we've got to take this in," Sy said.

"It's just what Eckles needs. Another reason for Lilly to murder Nels."

"So, do you know what she means by '…an abusive son?'" Sy asked.

"Yeah, but I don't want to talk about it. And the less you know about it, the better."

8:00 P

Dan gazed out at Fredrick Sound. The clouds, after lifting all afternoon, left a clear evening sky. The sun ebbed, tinting Devil's Thumb, the nine-thousand-foot peak on the mainland, an impossible wash of purples and pinks. He was remembering a story his father told him and the skyline went unnoticed.

Dan's dad, Martin, grew up on Sing Lee Alley playing with a Tlingit boy named Eddie Eddy. When Martin started kindergarten, he and Eddie spoke an odd blend of Norwegian and Tlingit the two boys had developed together.   Eddie's family moved a few years later. By the time he was a senior in high school, Martin was the BMOC – the smart, good looking basketball star who was going into University of Washington's new fisheries management program the next fall.

And then Eddie's family came back to town. One day, to the amusement of Martin's friends, a shabby Eddie walked over, shook hands and said hello to Martin in the Tlingit-Norwegian blend the two boys had created. Martin gave his hand a quick, dismissive shake, and turned his back on his childhood friend.

Eddie enlisted a couple of weeks later, and Martin Fields never saw him again. "That's one of my biggest regrets," his dad had told Dan. "When you're my age, you look back and realize you only have a pocketful of true friends in your entire life. You should cherish every one of them. I don't even remember who those kids were that I was trying to impress by ignoring Eddie, but I think about him a lot. What he's doing, where he is."

It was time for Dan to decide who his pocketful of true friends actually were. He needed to decide if he was going to stand by an old friend, or do his job; he clearly couldn't do both.   Lilly had screwed around on him when he was in the military, but did that erase fifteen years of friendship? She didn't have anyone now. No family, few friends. She was fighting for her life. If he turned his back on Lilly was he being a responsible police officer or a lousy friend?

And if he disobeyed the chief and sided with Lilly, he'd probably lose his job. He was getting too old to go out fishing, so where else could he work? Dan would have to leave town to find a job, and that meant leaving his house and his boys behind.

A raven's jagged call interrupted his thoughts, and he watched as several of the black, shaggy birds attacked an eagle trying to rob their nest. The eagle flew steadily upward, avoiding the ravens as they dodged and darted with beaks and claws. Dan had watched these eagle wars hundreds of times as a child. The eagles were strong and elegant, but the ragged ravens pecked and gouged to keep the huge birds away from their babies. The eagles were flashy, so they got all the recognition. But the ravens were smart, and they stuck together.

"Yeah, you should have known better than to mess with them," Dan told the eagle, as he watched the bully, now trying to escape the pursuing ravens. He listened to the almost musical *chinka-chinka-chinka* of the huge bird. "You even sound like a wimp," he added as he put his truck in gear.

Dan's mood lightened as he drove home. He laughed when he saw that someone had once again shot the "No Hunting" sign in Scow Bay full of bullet holes. He was still trying to decide if the city should waste money replacing it as he entered his kitchen and smelled the scent of fried Spam. "I'd rather smell the reduction plant," he shouted toward the living room.

"Dad, you've got to free your mind of forty years of prejudice and misconception. Someday Spam is going to have its own spot on the food pyramid," Jake said as he walked into the kitchen hoisting a fried egg and Spam sandwich. He had developed a love of Spam during his early days in Iraq.

"Why don't you eat bacon, like normal people?"

"Rocky called; he's waiting for a transport to Germany." Jake shook his head and laughed. "I told him that two of Nels' wives came in on the jet today, and he said he'd always thought Nels was gay."

"The crazy thing about Rocky—he comes out of right field, but sometimes he's spot on."

"Yeah, but this isn't one of those times. What's happening with the investigation?" Jake said.

"Did Heidi or Cynthia give you any info on the shoes?"

"You're going to love this. Heidi thinks tread is from a really expensive brand of shoes that are handmade on a kibbutz in Israel. I guess they're pretty trendy down south, but not the type of thing you'd expect to see around here. About two hundred bucks a throw and soft leather that turns to mush in water. A little too artsy for the Xtra-tuf set."

"I'll be go to hell. People actually pay that much for a pair of shoes?"

"Shit, Dad, look how much we pay for rubber boots."

TUESDAY, MAY 20

The Fisherman's Prayer

The Lord is my pilot, I shall not go adrift;
He lighteth my passage across dark channels;
He steereth me through the deep waters,
He keepeth my log.
He guideth me by the evening star for my safety's sake.
Yea, though I sail mid the thunders and tempests of life,
I shall fear no peril, for Thou art with me.
Thy stars and heavens, they comfort me.
The vastness of thy sea upholds me.
Surely fair winds and safe harbors shall be found
All the days of my life,
And I shall moor, fast and secure, forever.
Amen

Anonymous

8:00 A

Dan didn't notice his screeching windshield wipers as he drove into town. He'd obsessed about Nels Dagsen all night, and he was still exploring options this morning. Could Nels Dagsen possibly have been gay? It was easy to ignore

Rocky's comment, but there was that gay porn hidden in his bedroom. Still, the idea seemed preposterous. There was never a hint, even the tiniest whisper of gossip about Nels' sexuality. The scandals went in the opposite direction: he was always flirting with the most beautiful woman in the room. And he was macho—every minute he wasn't womanizing, he was hunting, fishing or playing basketball. He couldn't be gay. Dan slowed down at Scow Bay and continued considering the probability.

He'd need to call Lilly and ask her, but he couldn't quite get up the nerve. It wasn't that he'd been told not to speak to her, he really wasn't concerned about what the chief thought at this point. But it seemed like Lilly was starting to trust him again and he didn't want to mess things up by suggesting her brother was gay. He never could predict her mood, it was like a catch and release fishery: one minute she was reeling him in, and the next she was tossing him back. And anything could set her off. Especially asking her about Nels' sexuality. Norwegians didn't talk about that kind of touchy-feely shit. But at the same time, he'd made a decision. He was going to focus on proving Lilly's innocence. That meant risking his job and his future for her, and he'd feel awfully stupid if she kept treating him like a lower life-form while he was gambling everything to help her out of a mess.

It doesn't matter, he thought. I'm not helping her for her friendship, anyway; I'm helping her because it's the right thing to do. After a pause he admitted, Hell, I don't even know why I'm helping her, but if I don't follow up on this lead, then the *Urinal* is right and I should be taken off the case. With that realization, he dialed the phone. "I need to ask you something important, Lilly. You're probably going to think I'm crazy, but is there any chance Nels was gay?" After a moment's silence he added, "Lil?"

"Yeah, I'm here. I just wasn't expecting that. I've never really thought it all the way through."

"But you had considered it?"

"It's just that he always had a beautiful wife or girlfriend. It didn't seem like he could possibly be gay. But I started noticing this odd pattern at school. Derek Aaronson's kids always stay with his ex-wife when Derek's out of town."

"You think Nels and Derek's wife were—"

"No, just listen. This is such a crazy theory, but you're the one who started it." She paused for a response, but none came. "Well, Derek's wife is a mess. She sends the kids to school late and dirty and without socks or lunch money, so I can always tell when Derek's gone."

Dan parked in the police lot and waited. This was more than a yes or no answer, but at least it wasn't open hostility.

"A couple of years ago I started noticing that every time Nels was out of town, Derek's kids were staying with their mother. I kept blaming it on coincidence. I mean, what else could it be?"

"You think Nels and Derek were travelling together?"

"I don't know. I watched them anytime I saw them in public, and they never said a word to each other. But that was strange too. You know how Nels goes around slapping everybody's ass, but he'd look right through Derek like he wasn't there. And Derek used to deckhand for him. I thought maybe Derek was another one of Nels' disgruntled crewmen or something."

"You never noticed anything else?"

"No, never. But, Dan, at school there wasn't an exception. For over two years now, if Nels was gone, Derek's kids were staying at their mom's. I've kept track of that."

"Why didn't you mention it?"

"What? That Derek's kids came to school without socks whenever Nels was out of town? It's too crazy. Besides, there has to be some other reason, it doesn't seem possible my brother was gay."

Dan decided to leave his truck and walk to Derek Aaronson's place on Lumber Street. He needed to think. If Derek and Nels were secretly travelling together, there were all kinds of murder motives. Maybe Derek wanted to come out, or maybe he was blackmailing Nels. Dan didn't know of any gay men in Petersburg; he had no idea how the town would treat him, but it would be especially hard for someone like Nels, a life-long, aggressively macho bastard. People's reaction could be intense. Was his murder a hate crime? Someone who found out he was gay and couldn't tolerate his lifestyle?

Derek Aaronson lived in one of the newer trailers on Lumber Street, but Dan still had to walk around the usual debris to get to the front door. A stack of crab pots listed against one side of the trailer where moss darkened the grooves of the gray vinyl siding. Dan found Derek hanging gill net in the plywood wanigan and watched as he threaded twine through a loop on the bottom of the net, measured the distance from the previous knot, and tied a new knot in the web. Eventually he would have the heavy lead line— rope embedded with tiny pieces of lead—attached to the bottom, so the net would hang perpendicular in the water and fish could swim into it.

The hanging bench was old and swayed rhythmically with each pull of the twine. Derek's movements were graceful and methodi- cal, and he looked almost hypnotized until Dan realized that he was taking an occasional glance over at a small television where Judge Judy bullied a young man with a Mohawk and bad complexion. Dan tapped on the glass, and Derek nodded him in, still looping and swaying.

"Hey Derek, where are the kids?"

"They're staying at their mom's for a couple of days."

"You needed a break?"

"Yeah, I've kind of been under the weather."

"Too much celebrating over Little Norway Festival?" Dan asked as he considered Derek's puffy eyes and mottled face.

"Yeah, I guess you could say that."

"It almost looks like you're upset. Like maybe you're grieving or something."

Derek leaned over and pulled at the top of his boots as if the tide was coming in.

"Listen, Derek, I heard a rumor you and Nels Dagsen might have had some kind of relationship."

"What does that mean? Relationship? I crewed on the *Norge* for a few years, but that's not a relationship."

"Look, I don't want to pry, and this conversation is completely confidential, but I heard you were closer than that." Dan could feel his own face redden as he spoke.

Derek spoke calmly but his stare was cold and even. "Get outta here. Get off my property before I shoot you for trespassing. And trust me, I'm in a shooting mood."

"Look, Derek. I don't care if you're gay, straight, or perpendicular. I'm just trying to figure out who killed Nels; the guy deserves justice. If you fished for him, it seems like you'd want to help out."

After a long pause Derek laid the hanging needle on the bench and said quietly, "You're right, he does deserve justice."

After a lengthy stretch of encouragement, Derek started to talk. His alibi was solid. He and his parents had taken his kids to the Fish-o-Rama.

"Were you going to meet Nels that night?" Dan asked.

"No, we never even spoke in town. Nels was afraid someone would figure things out."

"How long were you two together?"

"A few years on and off. I don't know exactly. I fished with him for quite a while, and Nels was getting pretty paranoid. Couple a years ago I bought a gillnetter." He nodded toward the pile of gear to prove his statement. "Nels gave me money for the permit, and I started fishing by myself, so people wouldn't get suspicious. I still went out on the *Norge* when he needed help."

"Were you fishing with Nels when he rammed the *Tlingit Pride*?"

"Yeah. That was some crazy fishing." Derek tied another knot and sat in silence for a moment. "Me and Harry Tagaban were in the stern keeping an eye on the net. Man, there were herring everywhere; the water was thick with 'em. All of a sudden, 'Wham!' the boat stopped dead. It almost knocked Harry overboard. I saw the *Tlingit Pride* off the bow, and right then the *Norge's* engine just started to roar. I mean it was screamin'!" He shook his head and smiled at the memory.

"First thing I thought something had happened to Nels. I ran up to the flying bridge, and there he was, cool as a cucumber." Derek took a can of Copenhagen out of his back pocket and tamped a pinch of the tobacco behind his lower lip. "Nels pushed the *Tlingit Pride* out of the way like it was a bathtub toy. He never said another word about it. You wouldn't have guessed he was involved except he got so pissed about the insurance."

"What about the insurance?"

"Remember Nels started that insurance co-op about ten years ago?" When Dan shook his head, Derek added, "All the newer boats with good safety records got together and pooled a bunch of money for insurance. Then they didn't have to deal with the insurance companies anymore. It saved them big bucks, but last year they kicked Nels out of his own co-op because of the *Tlingit Pride* thing."

"If Nels started the co-op, how'd he get kicked out?"

"Roger Pepper kept pushing. Nels was so pissed. If it was Roger murdered the other night, I would have thought Nels did it for sure." He got up and grabbed a Coke can from the windowsill. "The *Norge* rammed the *Pride* and then Nels wanted the co-op to pay for the damages. I guess the rest of the members decided they didn't want to pay for Nels to go around ramming boats."

"Can you think of how that could have tied into Nels' murder?"

"Naw. Nels wasn't used to losing fights, but he lost that one." Derek spit into the Coke can and continued, "He had to get commercial insurance this season, and he wasn't happy about it."

"Did you know Nels was going to start a fish farm?"

"Yeah, that was our plan. We were both sick of hiding. Nels thought he could get a fish farm going, and we could move someplace where no one would pay any attention to us. Florida or Maine. Maybe even Canada. Someplace on the water."

Dan had to think about Derek's reply. Nels had actually cared enough for this man to pack up and leave Alaska. This was a side of Nels Dan had never seen. Never even dreamed existed. "So who do you know that wanted Nels dead?"

The two men focused on Judge Judy's next victim while Derek considered his answer. "Just a whole lot of women."

9:00A

Dan was morose. Instead of a new suspect, he had found the one person who was actually grieving for Nels Dagsen, and he felt bad for the guy. It seemed like this was Nels' one honest relationship; he had bought Derek a permit, but Derek couldn't even openly grieve. He had to find someone other than Lilly with a motive for murder. Derek didn't fit, but there had to be someone, and Dan had to find him soon; too many people were treating Lilly like a criminal. The chief wouldn't resist the pressure to arrest her much longer.

When Dan entered the station, he almost ran into Nigel Eckles who was draped over the dispatch counter chatting with Britta. "Well, speak of the devil," Britta said, twirling a lock of hair and smirking in Dan's direction. "Me and Officer Eckles were just talking about how you got your job."

"Well, good morning, Miss Britta. You're looking especially pretty this morning," Dan said as he headed toward the back room. "Hey Nigel, we need to talk about those footprints my son did."

Nigel made a quiet comment to Britta and then followed. "Well, you know, I'd like to take a look at them, but we just sent Lilly Dagsen's shoes to Anchorage, so we can wait on that until they come back. He was in the Army, huh? You sure can tell a military man, always in control, always in charge." He talked eagerly to the back of Dan's head. "That's why I decided to go to the police academy."

Dan entered the break room and pulled a plastic chair up next to Sy, who was spreading peanut butter on Pilot Bread. "Why didn't you just enlist?" Dan asked.

"Well, that didn't work out," Nigel waved a tiny hand. "But me and some buddies have a kinda club. We do war games sometimes on weekends, you know? I got a 'Peace is for Pussies' bumper sticker on my four wheeler." Eckles chuckled, his Adam's apple bobbing like a channel marker in a chop. "He saw some action over there, huh?"

Jake went to Iraq at the very beginning of the war. He'd witnessed horrible things that he was still trying to rationalize, and Dan wanted to insulate his son from those macho-by-proxy men like Nigel who liked to chat blood and guts for their own entertainment. His stomach twisted when Eckles started asking questions about Iraq. "Yeah, he saw action, Nigel. It involved living, breathing people—mothers and children and fourteen-year-old boys. But you know what? Right now he's making footprints. Footprints for a case you're working on. And for some reason, you don't seem terribly interested."

He glanced at Sy who handed Dan a piece of peanut butter-covered Pilot Bread intended to bog down his outburst, but the gears had engaged. "So let me clarify things for you." Dan leaned over the shaky table, pointing the large cracker at Eckles. "I don't ever want to catch you trying to get cheap thrills by pumping my son for war stories. You stick to footprints when you talk to him."

The chief, oblivious to the tirade, walked in talking: "Well, boys, we've got another bug in the Bag Balm. According to the Kake police chief, Marvin Brown is no longer a suspect. But, Marvin's crew has been threatening to get even with Nels ever since the ramming, and they've been vocal about it." He brushed crumbs off the dirty, white table and sat down. "Sy, I want you to take Nordic Air over to Kake and interview the crew this afternoon. Let's get this ramming squared away."

The chief scraped across the concrete floor in a futile effort to stabilize his flimsy chair. "The Wrangell PD found a man who flew into Wrangell on Friday. Name's Leventer. They have no record of where he went from there, but they sent us the security video. Dan, you're so worried about Wrangell, you follow up on that."

Dan ignored the double insult of the chief's tone and the assigned trip back to the museum. Arne should handle that. Still, the important thing was to find the ringer—the person who was going to get Lilly off the hook. He might as well look at the museum angle again; he didn't have much else to work on.

"Arne and I are going to follow up on the witness that was mentioned in the paper," the chief said.

"I thought it was plural. Witnesses."

"No, evidently that was just a tiny bit of editorial license. There was just one witness who saw Lilly running from Stadsvold Trail, and the editor is protecting the witness's identity." The chief shook his head in frustration. "He's a Mason and an Elk, and he still wouldn't tell me who it is. We'll keep on him. What else have we got?"

Although the chief was trying to put Dan on the fringe of the investigation, he still had the most relevant new information to report. Dan had talked with the two wives at the airport. There was no way Meera could have gotten to Petersburg from the Philippines, killed Nels on Saturday night, and then gotten back to the Philippines in time to be in Petersburg again on Monday. The flight took twenty-four hours from the Philippines to Korea to Anchorage and then down.

"Now Anya is a little more promising." Dan laughed as he told the story. "Nels took a restraining order out on her. That was before our time, but it's still in the books. He was afraid Anya would cause 'bodily harm.' The story gets pretty boring after that. She's living in Seattle, so she could fit the timeline for the murder if she could get in and out of town, but she already had what she wanted from Nels. They never divorced, so Anya got her green card. She knew he had remarried, and that her line on the money was questionable."

"Well, I'll conserve my opinion, but I like Lilly Dagsen for this one," Nigel Eckles volunteered. "It's time to question the wives, find out what they know about Lilly's relationship with her brother, and then bring her in for a serious interrogation."

"In Petersburg we don't call it an interrogation, we call it an interview," Dan said.

"Well in Juneau, when we're questioning a murderer, we call it an interrogation." Nigel turned his chair and straddled it for emphasis.

"Anything else?" the chief asked with a nod toward the Juneau officer.

"I hope we can keep this quiet," Dan said. "I don't see any reason anyone else needs to know at this point." The group listened with disbelief to Dan's information about Nels and Derek Aaronson's relationship.

"None of this information goes out of this room," the chief said. "If I find out even Britta or Arne knows about it, heads will fly."

The chief seemed interested in Nels' expulsion from the insurance co-op, but no one could come up with an angle that made sense. "I have to agree with Derek on that one. It seems like Roger Pepper would wind up shot," he said. "I want to keep it on our list, though." Then the group examined the handgun Sy and Dan had found in Nels' car. "This is the craziest case I've ever worked," the chief said. "We've gone from no weapons to a matching set of weapons. If Nels' gun is the murder weapon, we're going to have to start the whole case over again. Okay, let's get it up to Anchorage."

Dan had a second's lull to consider the possibility that Nels' gun was the murder weapon; that would take the pressure off Lilly. For that brief moment the cloud lifted, and then Sy glanced at Dan and handed the chief the suicide letter they had found in Nels' desk. Minutes seemed to stretch into hours as the chief slowly read and re-read the yellowed paper. "Did you know about this?" he asked Dan.

"About the letter?"

"No! Not about the letter. About the reason Lilly Dagsen's mom committed suicide. About Nels hitting her? And Old Man Dagsen not doing anything about it?" The chief's voice mocked as his face turned crimson.

Dan's silence confirmed the chief's suspicions.

"And you never said a word about it, even though it had immediate relevance to the case?"

"I don't think it has relevance to the case." Dan had to fight to keep control as he watched Eckles pick up the suicide letter and read.

"I could charge you with obstruction of justice!" The chief spit each word. "The officer in charge of the investigation." He stood, leaning on the plastic table and facing Dan. "I should fire you right now!"

"I'll step down if you want me to, Chief," he said.

"It's not your decision whether or not you step down." The chief was roaring. "It's my decision whether or not I fire you and press charges for obstruction of justice!"

"We need Dan's help, Chief." Sy, the voice of reason, slowed the tirade. "We're way too short handed, and I'm going to Kake, remember?"

The chief stretched himself to full height and gave his pants a hitch. "Get out of here. Everybody."

"Jake's footprints. You might want to take a look," Dan said as he headed toward the door.

10:00 A

Dan's parents had raised him with two important tenets: be conscientious in your job and true blue in your relationships. And here he was, ignoring both rules. The chief had hired him against everyone's advice, and Dan had let him down. He wasn't surprised by his rage, it was justifiable; so justifiable that he wondered if they would ever mend the rift.

But why was he disregarding everything that he knew was right, and risking his future for Lilly Dagsen anyway? She was the one who ran around on him. She hadn't even told him she was seeing someone else. He had to hear it from Yvette. Why am I banking everything on Lilly after so many years? He must have said it twenty times in the last couple of hours. This is the dumbest thing I've ever done.

What it comes down to, I'm ignoring my boss and the guy who was enough of a friend to risk his job and hire me, just so I can help out a woman who two-timed me twenty-five years ago. It doesn't make sense, but that's what my gut's telling me to do. I wonder how many cops have ruined their career by relying on their gut. Bet I'm not the first one.

He needed to talk to Sy, but his friend had gone home to pack. Dan had to keep out of the chief's way to avoid getting fired, so he headed up the hill to Earl Sanderson's to question him about the electronics on the old *Norge*.

A local committee had named all the streets. Those running parallel to Main were numbers, and those running perpendicular to Main were the names of old boats arranged alphabetically. The problem was that visitors didn't spell Norwegian. Earl Sanderson lived on Gjoa, called G Street by the locals. But if a visitor was told something was on Gjoa, they thought Gjoa started with a "J," so instead of going to G Street they went to J Street, where they found Jugoslav. If someone was trying to find Jugoslav they might look for Y Street, which left them out past the ferry terminal in the muskeg. Fortunately, Dan knew exactly where Gjoa was and arrived at Earl's in a few short minutes.

Earl Sanderson was a fine example of the theory that if a woman doesn't find you handsome, she'd better find you handy. An old four-wheel drive VW Rabbit was nestled in the weeds in his yard. He had converted it to a snowplow by adding a bucket from a four-wheeler. A faded for-sale sign was stuck in the back window. In spite of Earl's mechanical abilities, his old Norwegian house was badly in need of repairs. A porch ran the length of the front, but it slanted downhill, and the bottom step had a gravity-defying spring to it.

"Dang Earl, I could do a double back-summersault off that first step," Dan said when the old man came to the door.

"Who the hell are you?" Earl held his elbows close to his body, and gestured extravagantly with his lower arms and huge hands. His tiny, bright eyes nestled in a disconcertingly tiny, red face. Even as a child, Dan had thought of him as some sort of cross between a human and a king crab.

Dan's dad had brought him over once to see Earl's Christmas tree when Dan was about seven. The tree dropped through a trapdoor in the ceiling, so he didn't have to take it down every year. Dan remembered cranking the hand gurdy, a device usually used for hauling fishing gear but modified by Earl to raise and lower the tree. He reminded Earl of the visit as he reintroduced himself. "I'm Martin Fields' son."

"No shit? I haven't seen you since you used to play ball. I just got a bottle of Aquavit to celebrate Norway's independence. Come on in and have a glass." Aquavit, a traditional Norwegian drink, was supposedly hauled twice across the equator in the hull of a ship to develop the proper flavor. Dan's dad loved it, but Dan and most of his friends thought of Aquavit as rich-man's antifreeze and would drink just about anything else if it was available.

"I just wanted to ask you a couple of questions about Nels Dagsen."

"What the hell you wanna know about Nels Dagsen for? I don't know nothing about him." Earl pinched the welcome tight.

"And, ah, I wanted to see how much you were asking for that little snow plow out front." The pincers relaxed, and Dan entered a front room so full of flotsam and jetsam that he had a difficult time finding a place to perch. He finally sat on the couch and landed on a hoof from the mountain goat hide thrown across the back. Green glass floats were piled in corners—some covered with rope and some with barnacles. A large metal halibut tub was full of hooks waiting to be sharpened, and a rack of deer antlers held a spool of twine for tying halibut gangions. The only wall decorations were Fishing Co-op calendars, curling, dirty, and covered with fishing notations: *FSd, 3ch, 27, 4slabs, Sl W.* It took Dan a minute to translate: Fredrick Sound; three chickens, or small halibut; twenty-seven average size halibut; and four slabs, or huge halibut; at slack water, on December 3, 1977.

When he left Earl's an hour later, Dan wasn't any closer to finding a murderer. The rumor was true; Earl had taken all the new electronics off the old *Norge*, stored them in his basement until the new boat was built, and then put them back on the new boat. The top of the line equipment had saved Nels about $15,000 on a $200,000 boat. Nels had given Earl $500 for the job, and both men were happy with the transaction. Although Earl denied it, Dan suspected he'd been blackmailing Nels ever since. Earl had taken the electronics off the old *Norge* before it sank, which meant Nels had scuttled his own boat and scammed the insurance company. That information was worth enough to keep Earl in Aquavit for a while.

Dan was almost to his truck when he stopped to inspect Earl's old baby blue Buick. Its front fender, hood and windshield were seriously damaged. "A deer hit my car," Earl shouted from his porch.

"Shit, Earl, how fast was it going?"

"Not that fast, and it wasn't drinking neither," the old man said as he slammed the door.

Something wasn't quite right about the interview with Earl Sanderson, but Dan couldn't imagine how the old-timer might fit in. His initial thought was to check the files for an accident report on that old

Buick. If Earl was still driving, he could have gotten down to Sons of Norway in seconds. His only alibi, that he was knee-walking drunk at the time of the shooting, wasn't the best excuse Dan had ever heard.

He'd have to follow up on Earl; at the same time, though, Dan's biggest concern was, at least temporarily, keeping his job. If the chief fired him, he would have no way of knowing what was happening with the investigation, and he wouldn't have access to police resources. He'd wait to check up on Earl. For now the most important thing was to stay out of the chief's way. And come up with another suspect. He had to get the pressure off Lilly.

11:00 A

"Where's the chief?" Dan asked Britta when he returned to the station.

"See for yourself." She pointed a purple, acrylic nail toward the interrogation room where Nigel was questioning Anya as the chief sat off to one side observing.

Dan leaned on the wall across from the observation window and watched.

"Explain again how you make your money here in the United States," Nigel asked.

"I own dress shops. First just in Belleview. Now Redmond and Queen Anne, too. I design dresses and have them made in Belarus." Anya spoke matter-of-factly, staring at a spot just above Nigel's head.

"And you're pretty good friends with Lilly Dagsen, huh?"

"Lilly was always good to me."

"But her brother wasn't, was he? You were pretty angry at him if he needed to take a restraining order out on you." Nigel, seated in his trademark chair-straddle, was facing Anya and jutting forward aggressively.

"Yah, he's a kozel. He likes to have sex with everybody." She lowered her gaze to look him squarely in the face as she made this last statement.

"Okay, okay. We've established the sex thing," Nigel said uncomfortably. "So you threatened to kill Nels and then you left town? Did you go back to Russia?"

"How many times I have to tell you? Belarus, not Russia. I don't say you're Canadian. You don't say I'm Russian."

"We're talking about the murder here." Nigel shook his head as if Anya was clearly missing the point. "So where did you go when you left Nels?"

"I got my green card. I went to Seattle and started my business."

"And now you stand to inherit a bunch of money, don't you?"

"I want my free lawyer!" Anya said, standing imperiously.

"Sit down!" Nigel stood to emphasize the command, resulting in an awkward, chair-straddling stance that left him a head shorter than the high-heeled Belarusian.

"Both of you, sit down." The chief's frustrated expression would have made Dan laugh under better circumstances.

"So what about Lilly Dagsen?" Eckles asked when they were both sitting again. When he received no response from Anya, he repeated the question. "What about Lilly?"

"What about Lilly? That's a question? What about Lilly?"

"Did Lilly hate Nels?"

"Everybody hated Nels."

"So Lilly hated her brother."

When the questioning turned to Lilly, discomfort settle around Dan like a lead fog. He fought the temptation to interrupt, and then realized he had to leave if he was going to keep himself under control. He headed to the break room and was surprised to find Meera moping among the plastic chairs and wanted posters.

"Has Nigel already interviewed you?" he asked.

"No. I watched them talk to Anya for a while. Over and over, the same questions. Then that Britta woman says I have to come here. I'm too cold, but I'm not supposed to leave."

"I can find you a sweater," he said as he rummaged through his locker and pulled out an extra-large, hooded sweatshirt. "So what was he asking her?"

"He asked about Lilly; he asked about you and Lilly, are you lovers. He asked about Nels and his money." As she spoke she pulled the dark blue sweatshirt over her head and pushed up the sleeves. Her hair hung below the hem of the sweatshirt until she reached back and pulled it free. The resulting look was a tiny, life-size anime character in three-inch heels.

As he considered the new fashion, Britta stuck her head in the room and called Meera for questioning. Dan's curiosity carried him back down the hall toward the interrogation room where he watched, with amusement, as Anya walked haughtily out the front door.

Meera stopped at the restroom giving the chief and Nigel a chance to talk. "I figured that Russian wasn't going to help much. But I'll have this one talking in no time," Nigel said.

When Nigel began the questioning, he went through a physical transformation that Dan wouldn't have thought possible. Nigel beamed at Meera with a charming, boyish grin. "Are you sure you're comfortable? Here, let's move this table out of the way. We're just going to chat." He pulled his chair up next to Meera's and sat down.

Dan had underestimated Nigel Eckles. The Juneau officer was targeting Meera all along. He shook her up by bullying Anya, and now he was Meera's best friend and confidant. Hopefully she was savvy enough to see through the trick.

"So you're from Hawaii?"

"No, I'm Filipina. From Manila," Meera smiled at his mistake.

"I'm sorry," Nigel smiled sheepishly. "I hope I didn't offend you. I bet the Philippines are just as beautiful as Hawaii."

"More beautiful. And very warm. It's too cold here. I'm always too cold."

"Where are my manners? Let me get you a cup of coffee, I bet that will warm you up."

Shit, Dan thought, he's actually pulling this off. Meera thinks they're just having a chat. Even the chief looks impressed.

"It must have been hard for you—married, way off in Alaska with a husband who wasn't very nice. At least you had Lilly, though. I bet she was a real good friend."

"Yah, I missed my family so much, and Lilly was my sister." Meera ran her fingers through her hair.

"I can just see you two getting together and talking about everything," Eckles said as he ran his own fingers through his hair.

Dan felt like his entire body was going to detonate. Meera was falling right into Eckles' trap and there was nothing he could do about it. She was so innocent she had no idea what Eckles was doing.

"Yah, we talked and laughed all the time."

"I bet Lilly was the only person you could talk to about Nels, wasn't she?" He leaned forward, empathetic and concerned.

"Lilly understood about Nels. He was mean to her too. She knew all his tricks." Meera crossed her legs.

Eckles crossed his legs and leaned in even closer. "And Lilly helped you get away from Nels because she knew how nasty her brother was, huh?"

"True, true. We planned for a long time how to get even with Nels," Meera smiled, unaware of the dangerous territory she was navigating.

Dan put his hand on the door and was about to barge into the interview when Sy, carrying an overnight bag, grabbed his elbow. "What are you doing here? I thought you were smart enough to stay away from the chief for a while. And I really, really thought you were smart enough to stay away from the interview room," he said as he steered Dan to the car.

"I was watching Nigel interrogate the wives. I way underestimated him, Sy. He's doing the good cop, bad cop routine, and he's good at it. He's mimicking Meera's body language, flirting with her, getting her coffee. He's got Meera thinking they're best friends, and he's asking her about how much Lilly hated Nels."

"Well, Lilly's the number one draft choice. The best thing you can do for her is keep from getting shit-canned. Why didn't you deny you knew Nels' connection with the suicide?"

"I planned on it, but then when the chief asked, I couldn't lie."

The two men discussed Dan's interview with Earl Sanderson and drove past Earl's house to look at his damaged Buick.

"Well, I guess Earl is a remote possibility. Let's see what we find out from Marvin Brown's crew. I never really thought Marvin was the murdering type, but he has a couple of crewmen who I wouldn't trust." After a pause Sy continued, "So I told Rita your version of the breakup between you and Lilly."

"Glad you're not focusing all your attention on the case."

"She says you've got your head lodged pretty firmly up your ass."

"Why does your wife know more about my history than I do?"

"Because she's from the Eagle side, and Eagles think they know more than anybody else. She's right about one thing, though, it's time you and Lilly got things figured out."

"There's nothing to figure. Let's talk about something else, like maybe the halibut hook. So, you're Tlingit, right?"

"No, I'm Haida."

"What's the difference?"

"Haidas are better looking." Sy smiled.

"What about Rita?"

"Rita's good looking, alright, but she's Tlingit. She's Eagle from the Shtax'ta'chen clan in Wrangell. Glacier bear. You Weegians might think the Lutheran church ladies have a pretty elaborate social system, but the Tlingits and Haidas make the Lutes look like a bunch of marauding Vikings." Sy explained the Native hierarchy in detail. After the descent groups, Natives we're divided into clans like the Frog Clan or the Beaver Clan. All the families in one clan stuck together and helped each other out. If an elder didn't have any immediate family to go out hunting or fishing, members of the clan would drop off food from their own cache so the elder was taken care of. All of Marvin Brown's crewmen were from the same clan.

After the clans, the social groups broke down to houses, and, traditionally, each long house held an extended family. Grandparents, their children, and a whole slew of grandchildren all lived in one house, and that house would have a name too, maybe based on a particular story or its location in the village.

"Okay, so Sam Vargas says the important thing about the Raven Hook is that it's not a very nice piece of art. But it's a raven, so doesn't that mean something?" Dan asked.

"Nah, I'm with Sam on this one. There are some beautiful pieces at the museum. We call them *attu*. They belong to the clans and have been passed down for generations. Technically, the museum shouldn't even have them." Sy paused to organize his point before he continued. "Even if someone donated a piece, it wasn't theirs to donate because it didn't belong to any one person to give away, it belonged to the entire clan. Modern day museum curators respect that. So if we want a piece of attu for a memorial potlatch or whatever, we get it from the museum and then bring it back when we're done."

"Seriously? The museum owns them but they let you check them out whenever you want?"

"No, the museum doesn't own them, but it is a good place to keep them safe. And it's not as casual as you make it sound. Remember these are priceless pieces of art and culture. So, take Rita's clan, the Glacier Bear clan. They have a beautiful Chilkat robe up at the museum. When they had a potlatch in Sitka last spring, Rita and I went to the museum right before the ferry left at midnight and got the robe from the curator. When we got back to town a few days later at three in the morning, we drove to the museum, met the curator there, and returned it."

"I'll be go to hell. So how does this relate to the Raven Hook?"

"The Raven Hook isn't a piece of attu because it was found by a white guy, and it's a raven like half the Natives in Southeast Alaska, so it doesn't belong to a specific clan. If a Native was feeling criminal, they'd steal something more beautiful or more relevant to their identity than the Raven Hook." Sy looked at Dan, who was clearly confused. "I mean, when Rita and I returned that robe, I didn't want to. I knew I'd do it, but there was a part of me that kept thinking 'Why am I returning this to a white guy.'" He laughed as he admitted his misgivings. "Of course we returned it, but I could see someone stealing any of those other pieces out of the museum because they wanted it or because they didn't think it should be in a museum. But the Raven Hook? Can't see it."

"Sam says the only angle is that the hook relates to the Dagsen family."

"I'd say Sam was right on the money. Most people in the mood to steal a Native artifact would steal something nicer than an old chewed-up halibut hook that was just made to catch fish —you know, an Ed Kuntz silver bracelet for your wife, or a Wayne Price mask for the wall, or your great auntie's button blanket. But not the hook; it isn't pretty, and it doesn't have sentimental value, it has anthropological value—and it's deteriorating as we speak."

"Okay, so is it safe to say that the murderer wasn't Native because a Native would have taken something other than the halibut hook?" Dan asked as he slowed for the airport curve.

"Following that argument, you could say the murderer wasn't a Native, or an art lover. Now we're narrowing things down."

"I'll tell you one thing's for sure," Dan said, stopping in front of the blue and white Nordic Air hangar and watching Sy open the door, "I've never heard you talk so much."

"Maybe I'm Tlingit after all." Sy started toward the hangar, and then called back to his friend. "Hey Dan! Stay out of the chief's way. And Nigel's too. And maybe for a change of pace, you could keep your mouth shut."

"I'll have to keep my mouth shut, since Rita says I've got my head up my ass," he shouted to his friend as he drove off.

Rita's comment bothered Dan more than he expected. Why did Rita think she understood his relationship better than he did? It wasn't enough for everyone to meddle in the murder investigation. Now everyone was dredging up the details of a romance that was DOA years ago. Only a handful of people knew the details, but that didn't seem to stop the entire town from speculating.

When he arrived at the museum, Dan looked at the Native display with more interest. The pieces were beautiful. Everything was either in the shape of, or decorated with, stylized animals and humans. A narrow, bone spoon was trimmed with inlaid abalone discs. A mask of a bear had copper lips and eyes; its mouth was hinged so it could open and close as the wearer danced. The Chilkat robe belonging to Rita's clan served as the backdrop for most of the display. It was hand woven from the soft, belly fur of mountain goats, and probably was a several-year project. Chilkat weaving was remarkable because it was used to create the most sophisticated designs without the help of a loom. This blanket displayed intricate ovoids and geometric shapes in light aqua, yellow, black and white. Dan understood Sam's point about the halibut hook. It wasn't nearly as elegant as some of the other artifacts that were just as easy to steal. The presence of the halibut hook at the murder site seemed to be confusing the investigation, but it had to be relevant.

He finally found Marret in the back ironing a bunad. They scrutinized the airport video from every possible angle, frontward and backward, fast forward and slo-mo, and she just couldn't positively identify the passenger as the man who had spent time in the museum on Saturday. Dan would ask about hair color or build, and Marret would say, "I'm not sure, Danny, I think he was taller. Can we look at that last bit again?" He would spend five minutes trying to find the exact spot Marret was looking for, and then she would say, "Oh, I just don't know. Does his hair look blond to you? I remember his hair was blond." As he left the museum he realized with frustration that they were well past the important forty-eight hour mark, and he wasn't any closer to a solution than two days earlier when he first spoke to Marret about the Raven Hook. Actually, they were in worse shape; two days ago most people didn't dream Lilly would kill her brother, and now she was the prime suspect. Dan's investigation was going backward.

12:00 P

Dan headed to the coffee shop on a fishing expedition. When he walked in, though, the mood had changed. The guys who were anxious to talk *to* him on Sunday seemed more interested in talking *about* him today. No one waved him over to a table, so he took one of his own by the window and watched the action on Main Street. Three teenage boys looked in Knudsen & Holtan's window. They wore the low-slung pants that big city teens had adopted several years earlier, but one boy had made the fashion his own; instead of wearing blue jeans, he was wearing stiff canvas Carharts. As Dan watched him with interest, the teen walked a stiff, knee-bent gait that barely kept the normally high-waisted pants from dropping around his ankles. Petersburg posh, Dan thought. But he could relate to the absurd mix. The boy had taken an inner city style and a rural style and combined the two to make a totally, unworkable fashion. A lot like the police department was combining big city tactics and small town tactics to muck up a murder investigation.

Dan could monitor the comings and goings of the entire town from his seat at the café window. He watched Finn Pete slip into the liquor store and guessed they'd get a call from his wife soon. Normally he would head over and have a talk with Pete about the wisdom of falling off the wagon, but his mind was going in so many different directions that he couldn't bring himself to intervene.

If the liquor store was open, the bar was too, so Dan walked across the street for another visit with Yvette. "Hey, good looking, did you miss me?" He greeted his old friend.

"Hell yeah, but only because I wasn't aiming," she said as she carefully maneuvered her huge backside around a stool and dumped ice into a stainless bin. "Well, you're looking like the Norwegian Prince of Darkness this afternoon."

"So tell me something to cheer me up."

"Oh, honey, you don't even want to hear what I've got to tell you. That girlfriend of yours is going down. We just don't take kindly to murderers in this town. Can't imagine why. Especially someone as prissy as Lilly Dagsen."

"Lilly's prissy?"

"Are you serious? She's been too good for everyone since she graduated high school. She lives up in that funky apartment of hers and never comes out unless it's to watch Jake or Rocky do something." She slammed a can of Rainier in front of Dan and nodded her head. "Oh, yeah, trust me, everybody's noticed that. And she only hangs around with the teachers. She's been too good for us locals for years. And don't think people haven't been talking about you and this case. I swear, if she gets off, it's all gonna come down on you."

"You really think she did it, Yvette?"

"Does a bear wear a skull cap? I know she did it. Everybody thought it was Lilly, but then when Betty saw her on the trail, well, hell, that sealed the deal."

"Betty? Betty Hested is the witness? Come on, Vette, she was bat-shit crazy, even when we were kids."

"We're not talking about mental stability here, Dan. We're talking about Lilly running from the Stadsvold Trail to the Sons of Norway at the very time her brother was murdered, that's what we're talking." Betty had seen Lilly running, holding something that looked like a gun in the folds of her bunad. She hadn't even smiled at Betty, especially relevant since Betty was one of Lilly's mom's best friends. "And, I'll tell you what else. You have to stay out of this whole business. If you think people aren't watching you coming and going from her apartment, you don't know Jack scat. I mean it, Dan. This is for your own good; stay out of it, or she's gonna take you down with her."

Dan knew the town sentiment had changed, but Yvette's blistering honesty sent him reeling. For some inexplicable reason, he'd placed all his trust in Lilly Dagsen, someone he hadn't even talked to in more than twenty years. Now he was scrambling to save his own hide as well as find a murderer. And to add to the mess, how was he going to find the murderer when people were watching him as closely as they were watching Lilly?

1:00 P

Dan liked to take a close look at Alaska Marine Lines as he drove past. Barges came in piled high with eight-foot tall shipping containers. New trucks or modular homes were perched on a stack of five or six of these huge boxes. Checking out the newly arrived barges provided a little voyeuristic glimpse into the big money items friends and neighbors had purchased from down south. They were little puzzles: "I wonder if John or Netty picked out that siding?" or "Who on earth can afford truck payments on a monster like that?" You would get the answers in a day or two at the coffee shop or the hardware store, and it was never disappointing to hear the details. But today Dan took the curve at a distracted twenty miles over the speed limit. He wanted to talk to Jake before he met with the chief again.

"Hey, Jake. Did the chief take a look at your prints?"

"Yeah. He was pretty impressed, even if he did have to sort through a whole lot of Xtra-tufs to find anything interesting." Jake should have appreciated the chief's praise, but he was more focused on the case. "Things are getting too crazy, Dad. I kept telling the chief we didn't find Lilly's tracks anywhere, but he didn't care." Jake shook his head and rolled his eyes. "Last night Hank Bowman started joking about getting a lynch mob together and going after Lilly. Stupid stunts like that are only hurting the case, and the murder is all anyone is talking about. Nobody wants to hear anything logical and nobody is on her side."

"Yeah. Yvette says people don't like Lilly because she's 'prissy.'"

"Jesus H., *I'm* prissy compared to Yvette. And Hank, he fished with Nels and hated the guy. I don't think he even knows Lilly, prissy or not, and all the sudden he's forgotten how much money Nels shorted him, and Lilly is 'a money-grubbing bitch.'"

Dan decided not to tell his son that he was essentially eighty-sixed from the case. There was no need to make things seem worse, even if they were. A plan was hatching in the back corner of Dan's square, Norwegian head, and the fact that the chief was pleased with Jake's prints was an important part of it. He got a list of Nels' crewmen from Jake and arranged to meet his son at the memorial service that afternoon.

2:00 P

Like most things in town, Nels Dagsen's memorial service was scheduled around fishing. A lot of seiners wanted to get their halibut quota before salmon season started, and the trollers were gearing up for the king salmon fishery, so the service was scheduled for Tuesday afternoon. Even though this didn't give out-of-town mourners much time, it allowed the fleet to attend the service before they headed to the fishing grounds. But ever since the *Journal* had stirred the pot with Monday's article, it had merrily bubbled along on its own. The speed of the service, intended to benefit the community, had become another strike against Lilly. Some people thought the rush to get her brother buried was an attempt to hide something.

When Dan arrived half an hour early for the service, the Lutheran Church was almost full, with people already sitting in the balcony and the separate Holy Cross House where the service was televised. Dan scanned one face after another. Their old Sunday school teacher dabbed her eyes. Just down the aisle, two seiners sat with their wives. The wives looked appropriately long-suffering, probably because their husbands, with heads close to touching, were talking fishing at a funeral. Conventional police training would maintain that the murderer was attending this service, but it was impossible for Dan to imagine. Norwegians were frugal; they never wasted anything, especially a human life. It had to be an outsider that killed Nels, Dan thought as he looked around the church.

He'd always loved this building. Its elegant austerity hadn't changed much since his childhood. Tall, narrow, chapel-shaped windows made the vaulted ceiling look like it went on forever. The carpet was deep red against white walls, the dark wooden pews were smooth, graceful and soft to the touch. The one large piece of stained glass, *Christ in the Garden of Gethsemane*, was located behind an altar draped with a piece of white Hardanger embroidery that had probably taken some parishioner years to complete. The congregation was relatively quiet except for an occasional muffled snicker when the organist hit an especially sour note. If Nels had died of old age, most of these people wouldn't be here, Dan thought as he scanned the crowd.

The program had a large, smiling picture of Nels on the cover. It included a fairly short biography, a list of points scored during each game of his high school basketball career, and several other athletic awards and records he had broken. It said he was considered a high-liner in the seine fleet by the time he was twenty-two. Although the information would impress a sports enthusiast, his entire life's story was summed up in two categories: sports and fishing. The biography ended abruptly with "Nels is survived by his sister Lilly Dagsen." That was it. The short last sentence hung on the page like a condemnation; people would interpret the fact that Lilly was the only survivor as an indication she was the only one with a reason to kill Nels. Then they would take the fact that Lilly was the sole survivor, and add it to their growing list of circumstantial evidence proving Lilly's guilt.

Shortly before two o'clock, Lilly, Meera and Anya entered the church and began walking down the center aisle. The initially silent congregation began to fold in on itself like the rooster tail of a planing skiff. The three seemed unaware of the commotion, but Dan could clearly define each social group as people's heads pooled. After they were settled, Lilly stood and turned around. Every eye in the congregation looked up, hoping for some tiny clue or gesture they could recount at Emblem Club or Elks next week. Lilly simply asked for a hymnal and then, glancing with disbelief at the gawking congregation, sat down again.

Promptly at two o'clock the cannery whistle blew a long, shrill hoot. Lilly's head jerked upright, and she exchanged a glance with Nancy. Nancy's shoulders shrugged as she leaned forward to speak to Lilly. Others in the congregation reacted in different ways: some nodded as if they knew about the whistle, and some seemed surprised by the act. Dan was part of the second group. He could only remember a handful of times the cannery whistle was blown to honor the deceased. The gesture was strictly reserved for old timers, men who had something to do with the founding of the cannery. He couldn't imagine how Nels received such an honor.

When the pastor began the sermon, Dan didn't even pretend to follow along. He wasn't religious and, besides, Dan had played city league basketball with the pastor and knew he was quick to throw an elbow when the officials weren't looking. Instead of listening to the sermon, Dan studied the congregation carefully until the pastor asked for anecdotes. Sometimes this portion of the service was a total bust, but today people were eager to share stories of their fallen hero.

"Yeah, I just wanted to say Nels was a hell of a fisherman," one man announced. It was Hank Bowman, Jake's friend who had complained about Nels' creative math when it came to crew shares.

"Ah, one time in grade school," another man began, "me and Nels were hookey-bobbing and Nels' Norwegian mittens got froze to the fender of Old Man Sampson's station wagon." Hookey-bobbing— holding onto the rear fender of a moving car, usually unbeknownst to the driver, and sliding along the icy roads in a crouched position— was a favorite, although forbidden, childhood pastime. "Nels knew he'd get in trouble, so he snuck into the garage in the middle of the night and peeled his mittens off the back of that old Nash." This story led to murmurs of appreciation from the congregation, who understood the value of a Norwegian mitten.

The stories continued: Nels fishtailing into the ditch then telling his dad he'd had to swerve to miss a deer. Nels storing eggs for a year so they were good and rotten when he threw them at a teacher's house on Halloween. Nels getting hit by a sling shot when he went up for a lay-in at a basketball game in Kake.

"He sure could play ball," another man said. "His dad used to get so pissed. Oh, ah pardon me Pastor, ah, his dad, he got pretty upset because Nels would go through so many pairs of basketball shoes in one season. Just because he played so hard, you know?" As the speaker sat down, Dan saw him take a swat from an elderly woman sitting next to him.

Poor Jerry's going to get in trouble from his mom for cussing in church, Dan thought as he continued watching the drama unfold. Every time there was a pause in the testimony, people looked at Lilly to see if she was going to speak, but her face was blank and stoic. She showed no sign of emotion except for keeping her head held high.

Finally a local woman sang a clear, ebbing "Amazing Grace" a capella, and the pall bearers came forward. Somehow Lilly had managed to find six of her brother's basketball teammates to escort him to the cemetery. Two, who now lived down south, wore suits, but the rest were in hand knit Norwegian sweaters. Most of the pallbearers were typical for Petersburg, where people thought a Norwegian sweater was more tasteful than a suit, and where deck slippers were the dressiest shoes a man owned.

A dry-eyed Lilly, followed by Meera and Anya, fell in behind Nels' casket. Dan had never seen her look so vulnerable. It was only a couple of days, but her slim frame seemed almost skeletal. A few pounds made a big difference on someone as slim as Lilly. She stared at the back of the casket making eye contact with no one—nothing but elbows and knees in a baggy skirt and a worn pair of shoes. Her best dress and shoes, her Norwegian costume, was being held as evidence in a murder investigation.

Dan met Jake at the Sons of Norway reception. "I got to the memorial service about ten minutes early and they were turning people away. The place was mobbed," Jake said. As they talked, they circulated the large hall nodding to people who would make eye contact and ignoring those who ignored them. The crowd was sorted into the typical groups and sub-groups: three purse seiners here, four gill netters there, everyone arranged by their social status, or their pecking order, or their club affiliation, or their GNP. They heard a seiner say, "Well, Nels got me into herring seining, and I thank him for that."

Slides of Nels flashed on a white wall and Dan and Jake paused to watch Nels Dagsen at various ages and in various athletic uniforms tossing his charming smile at the camera.

No one seemed interested in chatting with the two men. "I would have brought a date if I'd known no one here would talk to us," Jake said quietly to his dad.

"You need to go over and say hi to Lilly." She was sitting alone. Meera and Anya must have decided not to brave the reception, and Nancy was frantically arranging food on the long tables. Jake grabbed Kim, the friend who had told him about the Fishing Co-op's missing gun, and went and sat next to Lilly. He talked animatedly until both women were smiling.

"Hey Sam." Dan grinned as he approached Sam Varga, the Forest Service anthropologist. "What are you doing here? I didn't know you and Nels were friends."

"No, I didn't know the guy. I was listening to the local scuttlebutt and thought you'd appreciate a friendly face if you were here. Didn't think you'd find many people interested in chatting it up with you."

"Boy, you got that right."

The two men discussed the halibut hook. Sam had done some research on that particular hook and was even more confused. The museum had several other more desirable pieces that were more valuable or more beautiful. Sam's theory was that the only thing connecting the halibut hook with the murder was Nels' father, who had donated it. "Either that or the thief was a halibut fisherman."

"There you go, narrowing it down to the entire town," Dan said with a laugh as he scanned the crowd. "Hey, Sam, I need to talk to Harry Baker before I lose him, I'll get back to you in a minute." He turned and began weaving toward Harry, but he was stopped en route by a group of women.

"Let's just ask him," one of them said loudly. "Hi Dan. I don't know if you remember me? Hal Teller's mom? Well, we were just wondering. I know it's none of our business, but we just couldn't quite remember: did you and Lilly date all through high school, or did you and Yvette go out your senior year?"

Dan laughed in spite of himself. "Mrs. Teller, why aren't you over there paying condolences to Lilly instead of over here gossiping about something that happened that many years ago?" he said as he continued swimming toward the permit broker.

"Hey, Harry, you got a minute? I just wanted to ask you a couple of questions about Nels' permits," he said, ignoring the permit broker's lukewarm reception. "Did he come right out and tell you he was going to start a fish farm?"

"Yeah, ah, you know people like Nels are pretty decisive and when he made a decision, he just really started heading in that direction full bore, and, ah, that's exactly what he was doing. And you know Nels, he woulda pulled it off, smart guy."

"So he specifically said to you, 'I'm going to start a fish farm'?"

"Well, yeah, ah, he said he wanted to sell his permits, and I asked what the heck was he doing, and he said he was going to start a fish farm in Metlakatla and not to tell anybody because it was going to make a few people pretty angry, and I guess he was right on that, huh, I mean...."

"When did he tell you he was going to sell the outfit?" As the two men talked, a timeline began to take shape. Nels had told Harry Baker he was going to put his seining operation up for sale about a week before he wanted the information posted.

"Who knew about the sale?" Dan said.

"Nobody. Nels wanted it kept quiet until the news came out on Thursday."

"Somebody knew about it, Harry. Rocky heard about it, and he's in Iraq."

"Well, my son Josh might have heard me talking."

"How many people did Josh tell?"

"Nobody – just Rocky."

"Shit, Harry, Josh didn't tell Rocky, Joey Olsen told Rocky."

"Hey, Josh," Harry yelled across the room, gesturing toward his son.

Dan watched as several people clapped eyes on the two men and began speculating about their discussion. Josh seemed oblivious to the scrutiny as he did a bow-legged jog to his dad's side, balancing a plate piled high with smoked salmon and halibut salad sandwiches. "Hey, Josh," Dan said. "I'm just trying to get a timeline figured for when you heard your dad talking to Nels Dagsen about selling his permits."

"Oh, yeah. Well, actually I didn't hear Dad, I heard Mom. You know how Bud and Nora have been looking for some IFQs for a couple a years now, and Mom was pretty excited to tell Nora that Nels was selling out."

"Thanks." Dan didn't even glance at Harry Baker as he walked away; he was considering the demographics of the rumor. The whole Baker family and Joey Olsen's family knew. Nora certainly told her husband Bud, and they discussed buying some IFQs with their accountant and the kids, and possibly even the crew. Then if each of them told, say, two people in two days, by Saturday half the town knew Nels was selling out. No wonder locals thought Lilly was the murderer. It was perfectly reasonable to think she knew about the sale, everyone else did. And it was perfectly unreasonable to think he was going to narrow his search for the killer by questioning the people who knew about Nels' plans. Everyone knew.

He was still hoping to find a crumb that would start him in the right direction as he walked to the tables of food arranged along the far wall. It was hard to imagine dishes so colorless were so delicious. Norway's four main food groups—butter, sugar, fish and potatoes—didn't make for a terribly colorful spread, but it was amazing how many delicious ways they could be combined.

He knew who had baked some of the dishes. There was his mom's cloudberry krumkake, lingonberry spritz cookies and huckleberry tarts. He piled several of those on his plate along with a huge serving of the traditional shrimp macaroni salad. Plates covered with plastic wrap were the harbingers of homemade lefse, a potato crepe spread with butter, sugar and cinnamon then rolled and sliced into soft, moist, gum massagers. Finally he found what he was looking for, home made bread spread with butter and thin slices of smoked salmon and hardboiled eggs. He grabbed several of these and headed toward Arne, who was sitting at a corner table near the stage.

"Hey Arne, mind if I sit with you?" Dan asked.

"No, ah, it's a free country."

"Yeah, that's what they say, but sometimes you have to wonder."

Arne, who had blindly worshipped Dan for years, quickly finished his meal and left Dan alone to consider how group dynamics could so effortlessly cause a fifty-year-old man to change allegiances. Arne's opinion wasn't Dan's only concern. He wanted to skip the afternoon debrief since it gave the chief an opportunity to fire him, but he had to attend. He couldn't miss a bit of the investigation until he found a murder suspect to replace Lilly. He looked across the room at Jake and Lilly. Her complexion was so pale that even her gray eyes looked vivid.

5:00 P

The chief and Nigel Eckles had already started debriefing when Dan stepped into the office. He hoped his entrance would go unnoticed, but the empty chair, stacked high with a retaining wall of folders and evidence packets, forced him to go find another seat.

As he maneuvered a plastic chair into the crowded office, the chief scowled at Dan and shouted, "Britta, call Arne. I want him in on the debriefs from now on." After an uncomfortable pause, he said, "Well, I'm having no luck with the identity of the witness."

"I think I've got the answer to that, Chief. It's Betty Hested," Dan said.

"Betty Hested. Dog gone it, I can think of more credible people."

"Okay, I'll need to talk to this Betty Hested ASAP." Nigel pronounced it A-sap.

"No, Nigel. Betty's an addled old lady; I think I'd better handle this one." The chief jutted his jaw toward Dan. "You showed Marret the tapes of the Wrangell guy. Did she give us an ID?"

"No, she kept saying she thought the guy was taller, and maybe he had blond hair."

"I'll send someone else to talk to her."

Dan could feel his face redden at the affront, but he was determined to steer the case away from Lilly if possible. "It looks like Earl Sanderson's been driving that old Buick of his. The front fender's a mess. I think we should follow up on that. See if he might have driven downtown Saturday night." Even as he said it, he knew it sounded feeble.

"I'm not interested in Earl Sanderson." The chief waved his hand as if he was shooing away an annoying fly.

"What about Roger Pepper? Has anyone talked to him about kicking Nels out of the insurance co-op?" Dan asked.

"Listen. The investigation has a clear direction at this point, and, unless Sy finds something nice and concrete about the *Tlingit Pride's* crew in Kake, we're going after Lilly Dagsen. Either get on board, or get the hell out. I'm tired of wasting time."

The chief presented the rest of the information methodically. Nels' handgun hadn't been fired in months. The gun the divers found was the murder weapon. Someone had chucked it off the ramp at the Middle Harbor after they stole it from Fishing Co-op and shot Nels. "So presumably the murderer is someone who was in the Fishing Co-op on Saturday, and on Stadsvold Trail and the Middle Harbor Saturday night." The chief looked pointedly at Dan. "The lab also said there's mud from the trail inside the hem of Lilly's bunad and on her shoes. But there's no blood or gunshot residue."

"That's not necessarily conclusive, though," Nigel Eckles interjected.

"No, Nigel's right. Since Lilly conveniently washed and bleached the blouse she was wearing. Twice. Not surprising we didn't find anything." The chief's glance challenged Dan to interrupt before he continued. "It was raining and blowing Saturday night and Nels' halibut jacket had a good spray of both blood and gunshot residue that must have blown right back on him. That's probably a good part of the reason Lilly's clothes didn't show much evidence."

The chief focused his entire attention on Dan as he continued. "The blood spatter isn't conclusive, but Lilly had a motive—a good motive—and she was on the trail Saturday night. And you might as well hear it all. They said judging by the angle of the wound, the shooter was probably left-handed. I guess I don't have to ask you if Lilly's left handed, do I?" the chief said with a challenge. "I'll talk to Betty Hested and Sy. Then we'll start working on Lilly tomorrow."

"I can start with the suicide letter," Nigel said. "That will break her down emotionally. Then we can discuss the information I got from the sister-in-laws. She's tough, but she can't hold up forever."

"You are not in on the questioning," the chief said, turning to Dan. "And I don't have to tell you, none of this leaves the room."

Dan could feel the blood pounding in his head as he walked out of the office.

7:00 P

The drive home was torturous. Should he disobey the chief's orders? The specter of Lilly's interrogation kept running through his mind. Nigel could break her down. Dan had realized that when he saw him working on Meera. Dan had underestimated the man. Lilly was already emotionally exhausted, and at some point she would stop caring and confess just to get away from Nigel.

Was it legit to tell her about the letter; level the playing field? And what if she really was guilty? The shooter was left-handed, what were the odds of that? And the halibut hook tied in somehow, and Lilly was the only person left with any connection to the halibut hook. And besides that, the chief had trusted him. Now here Dan was thinking of betraying his boss and friend. Was it unfair to Sy too? Sy had talked the chief into hiring Dan, and the chief was the kind of guy to blame his bad decisions on someone else. Maybe the best thing was to keep quiet and not say anything to Lilly. Have faith in the justice system. But it seemed like the justice system was on autopilot.

How would he behave if it was someone other than Lilly Dagsen? That was part of the problem. He had spent years taking care of Lilly, and now that his wife was gone, for some reason he was back to taking care of Lilly again. Was she really worth betraying his boss and getting himself fired?

Dan was still trying to decide if he should tell Lilly about the interrogation as he opened the back door and grabbed the ringing phone. "Hey, Lilly, is everything okay?"

"You were at the memorial service, what do you think?" Her voice was high and shaking. "All we had to do was walk in and everyone started talking, and then the cannery whistle blew; I couldn't believe it." Her voice rose higher with each point. "And the testimony. I had no idea what to do. I didn't even know if I could speak without crying. If I didn't say anything people would talk, but if I said something, they were just going to pick apart whatever I said. I couldn't do it. I knew I'd look guilty. I've never felt like this before."

After a pause for breath, she continued venting. "If it wasn't for Jake, I don't know what I would have done at the reception. I wanted you to come over and say something, but I knew you couldn't. I had to call you. I hope it's all right. I know we're not supposed to talk, but I thought you could tell me something that would cheer me up."

Dan didn't know how to respond. As much trouble as Lilly had gotten him into, well, as much trouble as he had gotten himself into, and the only thing that mattered was that she had wanted to talk to him. He needed to forget his relationship to Lilly and focus on what was important, and that was the fact that she was falling apart. He'd only seen Lilly lose control once, and that was when she was ten. She couldn't fall apart now when the investigation was focusing entirely on her. She needed to be rational.

Working toward his first priority, to calm Lilly, Dan decided to try for a laugh. "So, I'm at the reception in the middle of this crazy group dynamic where no one will even make eye contact with me, and all the sudden Hal Teller's mom has the guts to walk right over and ask if I dated you or Yvette during my senior year."

"That's the only intelligent question anyone has asked during this whole investigation. What did you say?"

Lilly's quick switch from the death of her brother to Hal Teller's mother startled Dan. "I didn't say anything. I might have had other things on my mind. Like, say, a murder investigation."

"Well, remind me to ask you again when this whole mess is resolved. Or maybe I'll just have Hal's mom ask you for me."

Dan puzzled on the silence at the other end of the line. He'd thought the story would make Lilly laugh, but instead she was turning hostile again. "We've still got a couple of angles we need to explore." He eased the tension by talking about the *Tlingit Pride's* crew and Earl Sanderson until Lilly started to relax.

When he told her Betty Hested was the witness against her, she was upset but stayed focused. "I saw Betty at about, I don't know, five or so. She was on her bike and I was late. I went racing down the trail and practically ran into her. But that wasn't at nine. You know how confused Betty gets anymore," she said. "And why would she testify against me? She and Mom were best friends."

"Yeah, but don't forget this involves Nels. If Betty thought you were the killer, she'd think she owed it to your mom to help find Nels' murderer."

Oddly, it was the subject of her brother's relationship with Derek Aaronson that calmed Lilly. "I don't understand how Nels always had a beautiful girlfriend if he was gay."

"Maybe he figured a beautiful woman was his best protection against discovery. I wouldn't want to be a gay fisherman in this town. He told Derek he had a plan, and if it worked they could move in together. Sounds like he came up with the fish farm idea so he and Derek could leave town."

"He must have really cared about Derek to take a step like that. Maybe Nels would have been a different person if he'd had an honest relationship instead of hopping from one loveless marriage to the next."

"I don't know. He might have. He had to spend his whole life proving that he was more manly than everyone else. He figured if he was a basketball star and a highliner, and married to a beautiful woman, people wouldn't think he was gay. I bet the paranoia was overwhelming, and he finally figured a way out."

"Do you think I could talk to Derek?" Lilly said. "I'm sure he's grieving. I'd like to talk to someone about Nels. Someone who honestly cared about him."

"I think it's a good idea, Lil. But right now we've got to focus on you. You have to pull yourself together and stay strong for a couple more days."

"I can do that, Dan. I'm feeling a lot better. You've always had that effect on me."

That stopped the conversation cold. "Listen, Lil. They're going to bring you in tomorrow morning for more questioning. And they have a letter."

At first Lilly rejected the possibility of a suicide note, but when Dan finally convinced her, she surprised him again. Instead of being upset, she was elated. "I don't know if I should laugh or cry. For thirty-, for thirty-two years, I thought my mother didn't even care enough to leave me a letter. To help me understand. To say goodbye. Sometimes I thought people were right, and my dad had killed her – otherwise I was sure she would have left me something. Either way it was horrible: my mother didn't care, or my father was a murderer. You have no idea what this letter means to me."

"But they're going to use it against you, Lil. They're going to say it gives you another reason to kill Nels. And they're going to try to wear you down. To get you to say something they can twist around. You need to prepare yourself mentally, so get a good night's sleep tonight."

"I can't sleep." She was half laughing, half sobbing. "I know you're going to think I'm hair-tearing crazy, but I keep dreaming I'm being eaten by a hamster. It's terrifying. He's rolling me around in his tiny paws like a hog on a spit and shredding strips of flesh off my body with his teeth. I think it's that nasty little Nigel Eckles devouring me alive."

Dan rethought the investigation long after he quit talking to Lilly. What had started as a plan to help Lilly had turned into open duplicity. He hadn't even asked her to fake surprise about the suicide note. The only way he could justify his behavior was to prove Lilly's innocence. If she was innocent, Dan was a hero, but, as Yvette said, if she was guilty, Dan was going down with her. He had to find the real murderer. What was he missing?

Dan grabbed a beer and plopped himself on the couch across from Jake in the living room. "I'm worried about your brother. Tell him if he can't get a quick flight on standby, to charge a ticket. I'll pay. I want him home." How had Nels Dagsen's obituary ended? "Survived by his sister"; that was the sum of the man's life. Dan wanted both his sons close when his own life was falling apart.

WEDNESDAY, MAY 21

You can tell a lot from a person's nails. When life starts to unravel, they're among the first to go.

- Ian McEwan

8:00 A

T hings usually looked better in the morning, but that was not the case for Dan. Insomnia had left him with most of the night to explore every possible facet of Nels Dagsens' murder. Thoughts clacked in his mind like rocks underwater— everything resonated, but nothing fit together.

And it wasn't just the case. He was obsessing about getting Rocky home safely; for some reason he desperately wanted both his boys within arm's reach. For the first time in his life, he was worried that something might happen to one of them. Jake had served three years in the Army, and Rocky had been in Afghanistan for most of his term, and he hadn't worried about either one. He was completely confident in their safe return. But now, for some reason, he needed to see them both safe at home. This case was upsetting everyone's equilibrium.

And Lilly's behavior baffled him at every encounter: one minute she was subdued and supportive, the next minute she was irate and combative. And that goddamn halibut hook. Was it possible the halibut hook wasn't even relevant? He had finally gotten to sleep by convincing himself that Sy would learn something concrete from the *Tlingit Pride* crew, but those hopes were squelched in the few, quick seconds after Dan arrived at the station.

"I got nothing from Kake," Sy grimaced an apology to his friend. "I talked with each crewman individually. When I got them by themselves, they didn't talk nearly as tough as they did with their buddies." He shook his head in resignation and continued, "They hated Nels, that's for sure, but mostly it was because they're so tight with Marvin. They were pissed that their skipper'd been disrespected. The money wasn't that big of an issue."

"It's nice to hear somebody still has some loyalty to their boss," the chief said, topping off his coffee and scowling.

"The main thing, though, is that they were all together on the boat. I tried to hammer a wedge into their stories, but it didn't work. They were playing poker, and they could all tell me the winning hands and who lost what. And it wasn't just like so-and-so lost a lot of money, it was specific, like Roy lost a venison back strap to three deuces, and Joseph lost a 2007, ten-horse kicker to a pair of kings. There's no way they could have kept their crazy stories straight if it wasn't true. And besides all that, they were laying outside the *Ethnic*."

"The *Ethnic*?" the chief interrupted.

"Its real name is the *Esther*, but everybody calls it the *Ethnic* because there are so many nationalities on one boat – Marco Gomez, Swede Haroldsen, Pasha Novakovich, Oscar Lumba. The *Tlingit Pride* guys all told the same story about trying to get the *Esther's* crew to play poker, but nobody could understand their accents.

"Anyway, just to be safe, I went and talked to Marco Gomez when I got in last night, and he said none of them left the boat. They would have to step over the *Ethnic's* rail to get to the float. Pasha Novakovich's a pretty paranoid guy and if he'd felt the boat roll, he would have checked it out, but the boat was steady all night. I'd be happy to pin this on someone from Kake, but Marvin's crew isn't going to help us any."

"Nigel interviewed the Fishing Co-op clerks again last night," the Chief said. "They aren't sure when that handgun went missing. Hooter hunting was opening and people had been in and out all day buying ammo and looking at guns. They were extra busy and extra short-handed because of the festival, so at some point they just started leaving the case open. They think the gun got stolen sometime during the day."

"That's crazy." Dan couldn't stay quiet. "They're retrofitting the facts to fit Lilly. The store was broken into. The only thing missing was the gun, so why would someone break in unless it was to get a weapon?"

"How about you let me finish?" the chief said. "When Joe Tall went to open up Sunday morning, the back door was wide open. He called the guy who closed the night before, and that guy said he'd made sure the place was locked up." He ignored Dan's frustrated sigh and continued deliberately. "Well, the guy's changed his story. He thinks he locked up, but he also said it's possible he got distracted and forgot to. The Viking Mobile was driving past as he walked out, and he crouched down to stay out of sight so he wouldn't get kidnapped." The chief drained the last of the coffee from his "World's Best Boss" mug before he continued. "The long and short of it is that now he's saying he's not sure if he remembered to lock-up, so the store may not have been broken into; it may have just been left open all night."

"So because some idiot forgot to lock the damn door, an innocent person gets implicated in a murder? That's bullshit," Dan said.

"Well, let me tell you the whole story." The chief no longer seemed reluctant to explain exactly how completely Lilly was embroiled in her brother's murder investigation. "Lilly didn't spend all day at the Fish-o-Rama. Sons of Norway had an open tab at FC hardware. She came and went several times getting things they needed for the setup.

She was in and out of FC all day." He spoke slowly and watched Dan as he added the most relevant information: "When we asked who might have had access to the gun case, the first person the clerk mentioned was Lilly."

"Jesus H. – of course he did. The *Urinal* named Lilly as the world's favorite murder suspect. That's the only reason the clerk gave her a second's thought."

"Here's what we've got, Dan. We've got a witness and evidence that both put her at the location of the murder. We've got a witness who said she had access to the weapon. We've got major motive. And we've got a left-handed shooter. *And*," the chief raised his voice to pre-empt Dan's interruption, "we don't have anyone else even remotely related."

"So can I even mention a couple of loose ends that no one is bothering to follow-up on?" As he reminded the chief about Earl Sanderson and the fact that he was blackmailing Nels, Dan looked around the room and saw the chief looking angry, Nigel Eckles looking pleased, and Sy looking like he wished he was elsewhere.

A flush was creeping into the chief's cheeks as he responded, "Old drunk is the relevant phrase. Do you really think Earl could have made it down to the trail and back home again without help? And with no one seeing him? And he wasn't at FC all day Saturday. No one could remember the last time they saw him there. He—Doesn't—Fit."

"Well, what about the halibut hook?"

The chief threw his hands up in exasperation. "What about the halibut hook, Dan? You tell me where it fits in."

That stopped Dan cold.

Dan's sleepless night had given him a new perspective on the case. If he honestly thought Lilly was innocent, and he did, he needed to forget about her. He had been spending half his time trying to prove her innocence and half his time finding another suspect. He couldn't divide his time any longer. He needed to take her completely out of the mix and focus on finding the real murderer. She was going to have to fend for herself for the next couple of days while he figured out what they were missing. It would be hard on her, but there wasn't any other option. No one was going to consider the possibility that Lilly wasn't the murderer until they had another suspect to look at.

9:00 A

Under normal circumstances, Dan drove Main Street; if he walked, it took him hours to get from one end to the other because of the small groups of chatters who stopped him along the way. Today he didn't have that problem. He got an occasional nod from the more stout-hearted locals, but, for the most part, he walked the few rain-soaked blocks to the coffee shop in an eerie, wet, solitude.

The scent of old grease and the hot, humid atmosphere of the Pastime Café wrapped Dan in an oddly comforting embrace as he took a stool at the counter. He nodded to Johnny Stadsvold, who was leaning his elbows on the counter, hugging a mug of coffee morosely.

"Hey, Low Floatin', I thought I might see you at the memorial service yesterday."

"Naw, Nels and I were never tight."

"That didn't seem to stop anyone else."

"I considered going for the chow. I figured Lilly would lay out a pretty good spread, but I don't know—that whole murder scene creeped me out. Maybe it got me in touch with my feminine side, or something," he laughed.

"Dang, Low Floatin', it's really not all that pleasant visualizing your feminine side."

"I said it got *me* in touch with it, I didn't say you had to get in touch with it." And then after a pause, "I don't even take the trail to get home anymore, even when I have to take a piss. I mean that's a serious lifestyle change. And every time I smell skunk cabbage, I get an image of Nels staring up at me. It gives me the willies."

"I don't suppose you've come up with any feminine insight into what the hell happened?" Dan tried to catch the eye of the waitress who was inexplicably preoccupied.

"Here's one thing I know, and I know it for certain. I don't give a flyer what anyone says, no local killed Nels Dagsen. A lotta folks didn't like him, but hell, I don't like anybody, and I'm not a killer."

Dan couldn't help but smile at Johnny's rationale.

"I mean, we've all known Nels was an asshole since he was in elementary school," he said. "He was an asshole, but he was *our* asshole, you know? We were used to all his shenanigans. A local just wouldn't have killed him. It had to have been an out-of-towner."

"Well, nobody else's theory is panning out. Maybe I'll try following up on yours for a while," Dan said as he slid, still coffee-less, off the stool. He considered Johnny's strange sociological theory as he walked the few lonely blocks back to the station. The small town knew its liars and cheaters and pretty much accepted them at face value. Would a local have killed Nels because of the fish farm, or would everyone just think that was typical Nels and tolerate it?

Dan walked into the station with a plan. "Hey, Britta. Can I get a printout of all the reports filed in the last ten days?"

"I can't do that without the chief's permission. I don't even know if you work here anymore."

"Well then get his permission." He worried the chief would say no, but Britta returned sullenly and began printing.

In spite of Dan's resolution to ignore Lilly's role in the investigation for a while, he couldn't resist taking a quick look in the interrogation room while he waited for Britta to finish printing reports.

"Your brother was the cause of your mother's suicide?"

"I don't know. There were a lot of things," Lilly looked down.

"According to the letter, you brother had physically abused your mother the day before she shot herself."

"Yes."

"And you wanted to revenge her death."

"That's not true. I didn't know about the letter."

"Do you actually expect us to believe that letter was in the family desk for thirty years and you never saw it?"

"I never went in that desk. It was my dad's and then it was my brother's." As Lilly responded, she examined her fingernails and tore a tiny shard of skin off her baby finger.

"The letter specifically says, 'I can't live with an abusive son.'"

"But my dad was part of the problem, too. If my dad had disciplined Nels for slapping my mother, she would have been okay." She watched a drop of blood form on her finger and then blotted it with a tissue. Dan noticed she had Band Aids on several fingertips. He had seen her do this same dispassionate destruction of her nails at her mother's funeral.

"We're not talking about your dad. We're talking about Nels. Your mother's letter said she was committing suicide because your brother slapped her. You found that out and you killed him."

"No, I already knew. I knew why my mother was upset." She examined her nails, looking for another fragment. "I knew all his secrets, and I didn't kill him."

"Let's talk about his secrets," Nigel scooted his chair closer to Lilly and leaned forward. "Yesterday Meera told me that you talked about what you would do if Nels died."

"No, we talked about how his estate would be divided."

"You didn't say you'd go on a trip when you got his money?"

"No, it wasn't like that. I mean maybe I did, but what I meant was if I ever had any money, I would like to go on a trip." Lilly tried to scoot her chair back to put some distance between Nigel and herself, but she was wedged in the corner.

Dan couldn't watch. He knew that Nigel's breath in Lilly's face would bother her more than anything else he could possibly do. Nigel had lodged himself in her personal space. This was the Lilly he had known thirty years ago. She looked so small and vulnerable. What if she lost it entirely? He grabbed the stack of papers from Britta and hurried to the back room.

The reports were the typical mix of small town infractions. Finn Pete's wife had called a domestic violence report in last night. That was no surprise. A tourist had reported a woman sitting on the Hammer Slough Bridge looking suicidal, but when the officer arrived, the woman said she just liked watching the clams squirt. The Petersons and the Smiths were still arguing about that Norwegian maple that kept dropping its leaves in the wrong yard.

The only thing unusual was an abandoned skiff. Someone had tied it to a piling at the ferry terminal during high tide. Whoever it was didn't know much about tides, or oceans, or pilings, or even skiffs, for that matter. When the tide ebbed, the skiff hung straight down, perpendicular to the water. The flooding tide completely submerged the skiff. No telling how long it had been there or if the chief even knew about it.

Dan called Viking Travel and got a list of all the businesses in town that rented skiffs: Ole's Marine, Scandia House, Karl's Rentals. He called each business one-by-one. And between each call, and between each disappointing rejection, he thought of Lilly in that room with Nigel Eckles and how similar she looked to the defenseless eleven-year-old at her mother's funeral. Focusing on her fingertips and the globes of blood she was using to block out everything else in her life.

Man, you used to be a whole lot more disciplined, he thought. Pull yourself together. You can't even think about Lilly right now. You're the only thing between her and a life in prison.

He refocused. Since he'd struck out in Petersburg, he began calling Wrangell rentals. That was when things started looking more promising.

"Hey Joe," he said to the owner of Wrangell Outboards. "I don't suppose you're missing any skiffs."

Joe was happy to talk to Dan, especially when it came to missing skiffs. He had rented a sixteen-foot Boston Whaler to a guy on Saturday. The guy said he was going to return the next day, but he rented for a week just in case. Joe hadn't heard from him since, and he wasn't quite sure how to handle the situation. If he'd had a definite return date, he'd report him as missing, but the guy's plans had been so unclear, Joe wasn't sure whether he should report him or not.

"I was nervous from the minute he left. He just didn't seem to know what he was doing, but he said he had plenty of experience. He was an awful nice guy," Joe said.

Dan gave Joe the call numbers and a description of the boat; it was a match. "Give me all his information and I'll try to find the guy."

"His name is David Leventer. He's got a Seattle driver's license, I'll just fax everything over to you."

Leventer. That was the guy who flew into Wrangell and disappeared. The guy on the video tape that Marret couldn't identify. The skiff fit right into that agenda. Had Leventer flown into Wrangell and then run a skiff over to Petersburg? At least Dan had the name of someone else in town the day of the murder.

A quick call to the airport got him the results he was looking for. David Leventer had flown from Juneau to Seattle on Sunday. So the guy fit the timeline for the murder, and it looked like he was in town on the right day. Leventer could have flown into Wrangell, rented a skiff and run it to Petersburg, somehow gotten from Petersburg to Juneau, and then flown back to Seattle from Juneau.

But when Dan turned his search toward the Lower Forty-Eight, he quickly struck out. The name Leventer was surprisingly rare. There was only a small handful in the entire country, and only one family in Seattle.

It looked like this was the family Dan was looking for; they had a son born in 1982, which made him the right age, but Dan couldn't find a trail. He didn't have a charge card or any of the usual electronic data used to locate a suspect. Finally he resorted to the Seattle phonebook and called Mary Leventer. She at least lived in Seattle and might have knowledge of other branches of the family.

Mary Leventer sounded like an older woman. She had a soft and curious voice. "Why is an Alaskan police officer calling here?"

"We're looking for David Leventer. I thought you might help."

"What's this regarding?"

"We're trying to locate a passenger who flew into Wrangell, Alaska a couple of days ago."

"Well, I have a son named David, but that wasn't him. He died of leukemia when he was ten. That was twenty years ago."

11:00 A

Dan couldn't think. The interrogation room pulled him like gravity toward its mass until he left the station and walked the length of Stadsvold Trail, hoping to find a small clue that had been missed. He meticulously combed every square inch on each side of the trail, ignoring the glances—either pitying or condescending—of people passing by. As he searched, he kept thinking about David Leventer. Mary Leventer's son fit the demographic he was looking for. He was the right age, right location, the only problem was fairly significant—he was dead. The fact that there was a nonexistent David Leventer flying around Southeast Alaska at the time of Nels Dagsen's murder meant that Dan needed to find him. But how do you locate someone when you don't have a name?

He'd have to try a different angle. Instead of looking for David Leventer he needed to find a guy in Seattle with a reason to kill Nels Dagsen. With that goal in mind, Dan dodged into the library, nestled snugly between Stadsvold Trail and the police department.

The Petersburg Library, located on the floor above the city offices and fire department, was surprisingly up to date. Dan wove around an obstacle course of computers and plastic egg buckets as he cursed, probably for the thousandth time, the architects who insisted you could build flat roofs in a rainforest. Ever since he'd been a child he had associated musty smells with books; the elementary school and the public library both had flat roofs that were constantly in need of repair. The odor had been comforting but the white plastic buckets, originally designed to ship salmon eggs to Japan, were always getting knocked over.

The librarian was one of the new breed, eager to help rather than just keep people quiet. She took him to a small, cluttered reading room that had all the *Petersburg Journals* for the last few years carefully sorted by date. He found the stack for the spring a few years earlier when Nels supposedly abandoned the old couple in Dixon Entrance, but there were no articles on the incident.

Maybe it really was a rumor, he thought as he thumbed through copy after copy of the *Journal*. Maybe the story was just Nels' crew trying to get even with him. He leaned back in the chair, running his fingers through his hair. There had to be another angle. Finally, in total frustration, he approached the librarian. She'd been pleasant. He might as well take advantage of her good nature.

"I work for the police department."

"Of course you do," she responded as if she was telling him, rather than the other way around.

"Well, I'd like to discuss something confidential if that's possible."

"Oh, no, I'm afraid not. Our readers are protected under chapter twenty-five of the Alaska Public Disclosure Act."

"No, I'm not interested in your readers. I'm looking for information on a boating accident, and it looks like the *Journal* didn't cover it."

"And it happened in Southeast?"

"I think so."

"We'll probably need to order Juneau or Anchorage papers though an inter-library loan."

"How long will that take?"

"Just a few days."

"I don't have a few days. I don't even have a few hours at this point."

The librarian thought for a moment and then smiled. "Here's what I'd do. I'd call the Juneau library and ask for Kate. She's a former Petersburg girl. She's working at the downtown library, and she could find what you're looking for in no time. Do you want me to call her for you?"

Dan was more than a little embarrassed to explain his situation to a Juneau librarian. "Ah, I don't think we know each other; my name is Dan Fields."

"Oh, you probably don't know me, but I remember you. I watched you play basketball when I was in elementary school." Kate laughed as she spoke, and Dan immediately felt more comfortable.

"Well, I'm looking for some information about a case I'm working on."

"I thought you were pulled from the case because of that *Urinal* editorial."

Dan's stomach twisted at the comment. "I didn't think news had made it to Juneau yet."

"Seriously? My mom has been calling me with twice-daily updates whether I want them or not. I don't know where she gets her information, but the town is totally immersed in the drama."

"I don't suppose you could help me out?"

"That's what librarians do best."

In less than half an hour, Kate returned Dan's call. "They are survived by a daughter, Neva Thompson (23) and son Steven Thompson (23) both of Seattle," the Juneau librarian read. "I'll fax the article to the Petersburg library right now."

His nerves jangled in a mixture of excitement and disgust. The story about Nels leaving people to founder in Dixon Entrance was true, but how could it tie in with a murder three years later?

This new information wasn't anything concrete, but maybe the Dixon Entrance story, along with the mysterious David Leventer, was enough to back everyone off Lilly for a while.

1:00 P

Lilly pushed past Dan as he opened the heavy glass police station door. Her typically pale complexion was blotchy and pink, her eyes puffy.

"Hey, Lil, you okay?"

"Oh, yeah, sure, I'm just great," she said, her voice high and quivering. "You go a few rounds with those bastards and see how you feel. Oh, but that's right, we're not supposed to speak to each other, and I'd really hate to compromise such a thorough and objective investigation," she ducked her head, shoved her hands in her pockets and started half walking, half jogging toward her apartment. She was angry. Hopping angry. That was better than the morose stupor she'd been in earlier.

Several people at the post office stopped to watch her flee down Main Street. Don't make a scene, Lilly, Dan thought as she made eye contact with a staring local.

She turned around as he watched. "I'll just head on home and wait for the arresting officers to come and drag me off to … wherever they drag people off to," she shouted.

Britta watched the drama unfold as Dan stepped inside. "Fuck off, Britta," he said as he walked past the receptionist and into the chief's office. He looked for a place to sit, but Arne occupied the chair that Dan had brought in that morning. Dan nudged a small square of floor space clear with his foot and leaned his back against the wall.

"We might as well get all the unpleasantness out of the way." The chief's look challenged Dan to respond. "We're going to arrest Lilly tomorrow."

"Listen, Chief," Dan had been practicing this speech since he left the library. "That guy named Leventer who flew into Wrangell." He tried to sound rational, but he sounded desperate, even to himself as he explained the swamped skiff and the article about the abandoned elderly couple. "We still need to follow up on some loose ends—I mean that's a motive for murder if I ever heard one."

"You're grasping, Dan. That was three years ago. Why would someone wait and deal with it now?" The chief rolled his eyes as if he was talking to a child, rather than a fellow police officer.

It took every bit of Dan's self-control to continue as he relayed the information he had discovered about David Leventer. "Can we just hold off on Lilly's arrest until we get some of this squared away?"

The chief pronounced each word slowly, punctuating with a jabbing index finger. "You have completely lost your objectivity. We need to act on this before Lilly starts settling Nels' estate. Then she becomes a serious flight risk. Get a grip."

Dan felt every nerve sputter and misfire as the chief continued. "Now, here's what's going to happen: You're going to drive Nigel to the airport and put him on the afternoon flight. Then you're going to come back here and start working on a stack of paperwork that we've been ignoring for the last few days."

Dan was silent.

"Sy's agreed to go pick up Lilly in the morning," the chief continued. "Judge Hasselburg will come in on the early jet. We'll get Lilly arraigned and out on bail, and the judge can head home on the afternoon jet. Lilly won't even have to spend the night in jail. That's the best we can do. I'll see you when you get back from the airport." The chief thanked Nigel Eckles for his help, shook his hand and dismissed the two men with a nod.

Dan expected a glower from Britta as he passed her desk, but she seemed surprisingly content. He understood her self-satisfaction when Nigel Eckles stopped for a minute, took out a card, wrote his home phone number on the back, and tucked it in Britta's palm.

"See you soon, Nige," the receptionist said as the two men left the station.

"Boy, that Britta's really something," Eckles said.

Their ride to the airport was silent. If Dan opened his mouth, a mass of roiling anger would rush out. Eckles had been brought to Petersburg to help solve a crime. Instead he had managed to find himself a girlfriend and convince the chief that an innocent person was guilty.

Dan applied Low Floatin' Johnny's murder theory to Nigel Eckles: Nigel's an asshole, but he's not our asshole, he thought. He controlled his anger by noting the similarities between Nigel and small rodents; his quick, feral eyes and even his prominent nose and recessive chin added to the effect. He had his tiny hands perched on each side of his carry-on bag as if he were hugging a crunchy new hamster treat.

2:00 P

The airport was deserted. A couple of travelers scanned the overcast sky nervously and wondered if visibility was getting too low for the jet to land, while the TSA agent, Ray Hatfield, stood at a stainless counter going through luggage. Ray had been a fairly slow-moving janitor at the high school until he was fired for stealing tools from the shop class. Unfortunately, the administration had decided not to press charges. That would have embarrassed Ray's parents. Now he was working for TSA.

"Lilly Dagsen is a murder suspect, and Ray Hatfield has a government security job," Dan said to Eckles. "If that's the American justice system, I think I'll move to Canada." And with that he headed back to the station.

The chief hadn't exaggerated about the mountain of paper work. Dan started sorting through the stacks, but his mind kept travelling back to the abandoned couple in Dixon Entrance. If the chief wasn't going to follow up on it, he would. Unfortunately, the name Thompson was a lot more common than Leventer. There were three Neva Thompsons in the Seattle area. One was three, one was eighty-two, and one, a twenty-six year old, was in a secure mental institution. Was that the couple's daughter?

But there were twenty-eight Steven Thompsons in the Pacific Northwest. Mucking through twenty-eight Steven Thompsons was going to take all afternoon, and if the chief figured out what he was doing, things would get ugly. But hell, things already were ugly. He split his time between searching records and looking over his shoulder, making sure no one was watching. At least he didn't have to worry about Eckles anymore.

As he searched birth certificates by county, he worried. He worried about Lilly's interview and wished he could talk to Sy about it. But he also worried about getting Sy in trouble. And he worried about Lilly and if he should call her. He worried about how much research he could get done before he was fired. And mostly he worried about Steven Thompson. What if he hadn't been born in the Northwest? If that were the case, his entire search was useless. And what could he do then?

After hours of work, Dan had eliminated twenty-six Thompsons by age. If he'd found the right Neva Thompson, her brother would also be twenty-six, and he had two, twenty-six-year-old Steven Thompsons in the Seattle area.

This whole search could be a dead end. Even if Dan found the right Steven Thompson, they would still have to somehow tie Thompson to Leventer to place him in Petersburg. The chief was right, he was flailing.

Dan paced the length of the police department. It looked like everyone had gone home except the evening dispatcher. He closed his office door and looked up the phone number for the Seattle PD.

Shit, if I could get in any more trouble, this is how to do it, he thought as he called Seattle. What's the worst that could happen? Seattle will call here tomorrow and tell the chief, and the chief will shit-can me. That's probably going to happen anyway, so I might as well go with both feet in.

A Seattle police officer interrupted his thoughts. "Yeah, ah, this is Officer Dan Fields of the Petersburg Police Department here in Alaska. We have two suspects that we need questioned regarding a murder that took place a few days ago."

8:00 P

Dan continued puzzling about Steven Thompson as he drove home. He flipped his windshield wipers on high to get a better view of a halibut boat in the Narrows. The boat was running with the tide, and he could see orange and lime green oil skinned deckhands coiling gear on deck. "Hey Jake," he hollered as he walked into his kitchen. "Did you see how fast that boat's running with the tide? I bet it's going about sixteen-eighteen knots."

"I saw it. Why are they headed south? Seems like a halibut boat would be running toward Frederick Sound."

When their discussion turned to the day's events, Dan's sense of foreboding escalated. The investigation would start a new phase tomorrow. After Lilly's arrest his focus would change from finding a different suspect to proving her innocence. The chief no longer trusted his judgment, so everything he did would be questioned. That is unless he was fired outright.

He could still expect some kind of disciplinary action for not telling the chief about Nels' part in the suicide. And what about the interrogation? Had the chief figured out that Lilly knew about the letter? That would get him fired for sure, but at this point he didn't even care. He didn't care about his job or his reputation or his friends. All he could think about was solving the case. They were missing something and sitting around worrying about it wasn't helping anybody. Dan slammed his recliner into the upright position and leaned forward. "I'm heading over to Lilly's."

"I can't believe it took you this long," Jake clearly approved. "Are you sure that's what you want to do? You can kiss your job goodbye if you go."

"Hell, you could use some cheap labor working on your place, right? But I'm warning you right now, I don't take directions very well."

"So, he finally admits he's uncoachable. That's the first step toward conquering your shortcomings." Jake grinned as Dan grabbed keys and walked out the door.

9:00 P

Dan plodded up Lilly's apartment stairs, his eyes wandering from the tattered, green shingles tacked carelessly on each step, down to the oil tank and skunk cabbage competing for territory below. How did it come to this? he wondered. How did Lilly Dagsen, one of the sweetest, prettiest, richest girls in Petersburg, wind up living in this funky apartment over a drugstore? His thoughts were interrupted when he saw Lilly's silhouette at the top of the stairs.

"Dan? I didn't realize it was you. You usually sound like the cavalry charging up those stairs."

"Twenty-four steps," he said as he walked into her kitchen.

"Yeah, I know. I count them every time I use them."

"Every sack of groceries, every pot of flowers—everything you've packed into this apartment you've carried up twenty-four steps."

A series of worry lines appeared between Lilly's brows as she watched him kick off his boots and settle on the couch. "I thought we weren't going to see each other until the case was squared away. What's going on?"

"We need to talk. The case isn't going good, and I'm worried." He looked at Lilly's hands as he spoke. Every one of her fingertips was covered with a Band-Aid.

"It's not as bad as it looks," she said, sitting on the couch and tucking her fingertips under her thighs. "Some of the Band-Aids are just keeping me from making things worse." She shifted self-consciously. "I'm worried about you, though. The chief will fire you for sure if he finds out you've been over here. You should go home. The case will sort itself out."

"Christ on a bicycle, Lilly. You always think things'll sort themselves out. That's your answer to everything."

Right as he was making the decision to openly disobey the chief because things were going so badly, Lilly was deciding things were fine. He tried to get the frustrated tirade under control, but couldn't. "Your dad leaves you penniless, and you wait twenty years for things to sort themselves out. When are you going to start sticking up for yourself?"

"I stick up for myself when I think it matters, Dan. That's when I stick up for myself. The little hamster man has gone back to Juneau; things'll settle down now. But what I don't understand—what I'd really like to get my mind around—is what gives you the right to thump up those twenty-four steps and tell me how to handle my life? You walked away from that right years ago, and I haven't seen a thing change since the day you came moseying back into town with that hot little wife of yours."

"Okay, okay. You're right; I'm sorry. This whole investigation is making me crazy."

"Making you crazy? I'm the suspect!"

"I said I'm sorry, Lilly. You're right, we've both got to calm down. We need to talk."

Lilly sat studying his face for a moment, and then said, "Something bad's happened, hasn't it?"

"Yeah, something real bad." Dan paused for a moment as his gaze took in the overstuffed furniture, so threadbare it almost looked like leather, the worn rug that had been turned several times to evenly distribute the bare spots, and the open window intended to combat the excessive heat. Lilly had done everything possible to make this a comfortable home, but there was only so much you could do with an eighty-year-old apartment and no money. And now he had to give her another punch in the gut. "Hamster man recommended your arrest. The chief's sitting on it overnight, but he doesn't have any options. You're the only person who looks good for it, and you look awfully darn good."

"That's crazy! Why now? Why would I suddenly, after twenty complacent years, murder my brother?"

"The reports came back from the Anchorage lab. Your shoes and bunad both had mud from Stadsvold Trail on them."

"Of course they did. I took the trail over and over again that afternoon!"

"And the shooter was left handed. And your brother was going to sink all your money into a fish farm. They've exhausted every other option, Lilly. No one else makes sense. The chief's got to do something. He asked for Nigel's help. Now that Nigel's made his recommendation, the chief can't just ignore it."

"My god, everyone is looking at me like I'm a leper. People I've worked with for years are avoiding me. If I go in the teachers' room, everyone stops talking. You saw how people stared at me on Main Street today. And now I'm actually going to be arrested? This is unreal.

"Why are you here?" Her voice rose.

"I came to talk to you." Dan looked her squarely in the eyes. "We need to go over everything. We're missing something somewhere, and we've got to figure out what it is."

"But we've already been through this." Lilly ran a hand through her hair and then glanced from one side of the room to the other as if she had suddenly been dropped into a foreign country.

"We need to figure out who killed your brother, Lilly. And we need to do it tonight. Otherwise you're going to jail. You know more about him than anyone else does. We've got to go over everything systematically. The only way to keep you out of jail is to figure out who shot Nels," he said.

Lilly pulled her knees to her chest and wrapped her arms around her legs. Dan watched her with concern. She wore a long-sleeved, fitted tee tucked into ancient Carharts; a pair of old Xtra-tufs, cut down and rosemalled, covered her feet. How could someone look so friggin beautiful in a pair of old, beat up canvas pants, Dan wondered.

Lilly took a moment to compose and then returned to the conversation. "Well, I doubt this is going to help my case any, but I did figure out one thing that's been bothering me since my mom died. I think I understand why Nels slapped my mother that day." She paused to be sure she had Dan's full attention and then continued. "He had this really good friend—Erik somebody. When school got out Nels talked

Dad into taking Erik out on the boat. Nels was getting a full crew share that summer, but after some serious negotiating on Nels' part, Dad agreed to take Erik out for a half-share." Lilly was so excited she stood and started pacing.

"Those two boys were inseparable. Everyone called them 'the twins' because you never saw one without the other. They got in from fishing and Nels came home to get cleaned up. Then he was going to spend the night at Eric's." She stopped for a moment, as if visualizing the scene. "Mom said no. School was going to start, and Nels needed to get back on a regular schedule. They had a huge argument.

"Dad was sleeping after the opening and Mom was worried that Nels would wake him up with his shouting, so she was kind of whispering in a low voice. Then Nels would shout an answer. He knew Dad would overrule Mom and let him go to Erik's, so he was talking loud to wake him up. Mom was afraid of what would happen if Dad woke up, so she was frantically trying to keep Nels quiet." Tears started falling as Lilly recounted that terrible day. "Mom said something like, 'You'd think you two were in love,' or something like that. She was just joking, but Nels lost it.

"I could never figure out what triggered that rage, but now it makes sense. I bet his feelings toward Erik terrified him."

"You really think he knew that long ago?" Dan said.

"He may not have known he was gay, but I bet he thought Mom was hinting there was something odd about their relationship."

They were far enough off topic that when Lilly said she was hungry, Dan was happy to join her in a snack. "Meera made me a huge batch of lumpia," Lilly offered as she went into the kitchen. "And adobo. And I know you like adobo."

She walked back balancing two huge plates of lumpia and adobo that managed to elevated the mood, bite by bite. The two spent hours discussing every possible facet of the case except Dan's theory about the couple in Dixon Entrance. With all the turmoil in Lilly's life, he didn't have the heart to tell her that Nels really had abandoned the elderly couple that was asking him for help.

As they talked, a sense of warmth and equanimity overtook the pair. "I guess the one good thing about all this is that we're back to being friends again. With Nels gone, I don't have anybody but Nancy and now, you. No family, two friends. That's the grand total after an entire life in this little town."

"I don't want to sound like the insensitive guy I am, but I don't understand." Dan's response trailed off.

"Don't understand what?"

"Well, what happened to all your friends? I mean you had so many friends in high school, but when I got out of the Army, it seemed like you mostly kept to yourself."

Lilly looked up in disbelief. "Even if you're not insensitive, you're definitely clueless. You honestly don't know what happened to all my friends?" When she saw his confusion, she continued, "Your good buddy Yvette took care of them. She mounted a pretty serious smear campaign while I was in Norway."

"Smear campaign? You can't be serious?"

"Actually, the psychology involved is pretty interesting. Yvette was either incredibly calculating or she actually believed what she wrote."

"Like what did she write?"

"Well, first Sherri Windrum quit writing to me. After a while I wrote and asked her what was going on and she wrote back and said that I had told mutual friends that she wasn't very smart and would never make it through college." Lilly started to bite a fingernail and then remembered her fingertips were covered.

"Then April Hested quit writing. Same thing, I wrote to her, she wrote a nasty letter back saying I had always flirted with her boy-friend when she wasn't around."

"But why do you think it was Yvette?"

"Whenever I could get to the bottom of things, it was always Yvette who had told someone something. Think about it. You two hung out for that entire year after you got busted with the journalism keys. She was completely and totally in love with you."

Dan started thinking back to Yvette's innuendos. "I was clueless," he said. They had gone to prom together, but just as friends. And she did always have a little something snide to say about Lilly.

"And you wonder why Hal Teller's mom asked you who you were going out with in your senior year? You and Yvette were so tight people thought you were a couple."

"We were just buddies!" Dan's disbelief was turning to anger.

"And, you know, if you followed the rumor-mill in this murder investigation, I think you'd find Yvette has been pretty busy."

"She couldn't hold a grudge that long." He knew he was wrong as he said the words. "Why didn't you ever tell me?"

"I didn't want to upset you when I came back from Norway. You were going into the Army in a couple of months, and I figured it wouldn't matter. And I just wanted a perfect couple of months."

"It was pretty perfect, too. Wasn't it?"

"Yeah, it was perfect in every way," she smiled. "And then you left, and we never talked again."

"And whose fault was that?" Dan asked. "There's no way you'll pin that one on me."

"Well then who should I pin it on? You ditched me, but good."

"Oh, no, I'll take the blame for Yvette, but the split was your fault. You hooked up with C.J. Schwartz as soon as I left town."

"You're not serious! C.J. and I hung around some; that was it. I only had a couple of good girlfriends left, and they went off to college. I was still friends with most of the guys because they didn't gossip with Yvette, but they all started fishing year round. C.J. got a job at the bank, so he was pretty much the only person left in town for me to hang out with."

"Everybody told me you two were going out."

"I told you we weren't, Dan, but you didn't believe me," Lilly snapped. "And who was everybody, anyway? Yvette?"

The two sat in an affirmative silence for several beats before Dan responded, "You and C.J. were together all the time."

"Yeah, a lot like you and Yvette were together all the time when I was in Norway. But the difference is, I trusted you."

"But even the Army kept telling us to forget the girl back home because she wasn't going to wait around."

"So you raced right out and found someone else. That was a pretty quick fix."

"That's not fair. I didn't meet Emily until about six months before I got out. I just laid low for a couple of years, and then I started thinking about coming home and seeing you with other guys, and I decided I wanted to find someone else before I came back. But what about you? Why didn't you find someone else?"

"Uff da – in Petersburg? You know the kind of guys who come to town. Construction workers who are looking for a fling, Forest Service who are already married, or deckhands who are looking for drugs."

"It-sha, I can't believe I mucked things up so badly, Lilly." Dan looked out the window to avoid her gaze.

"It takes us twenty-some years to get our high school romance straightened out, and now I'm going to jail for murder, so it doesn't even matter."

She paused for a moment and then looked Dan straight in the eyes. "Listen, Dan, I don't want you to go in tomorrow."

"In where? To the station?"

"Yes, the station. I don't want you there when I'm arrested."

"Of course I'll be there. I don't want you going through that on your own. You'll need a friend."

"Sy will be supportive; he's always been sweet to me. I mean it Dan. You seeing me in hand cuffs—I'll fall apart."

"It won't be bad, Lilly. The chief's got things figured out so it's all going to go pretty fast."

"You say I'm a Pollyanna, and then you tell me that getting arrested for murder isn't going to be bad? It will be the biggest humiliation of my life. Everyone will know. Everyone probably already knows. I can't stand the thought of you being there to witness it all."

Dan wasn't sure how to respond. He needed time to think. Finally he decided to try a distraction. "At least Nigel isn't going to be there. That would make things even worse." When Lilly didn't comment, he continued, "You know, every time you call Nigel a hamster, I get this visual of Jack Nicholson in that movie—*Shining*, or something like that. He curls up his lip and makes this little rat-chewing gesture with his mouth that I can't get out of my mind. Did you ever see that movie?"

"No, I don't think so."

"Well, let's watch it when life is back to normal."

"I'd like that."

Dan wanted to touch her. He was desperate to put his arm around her and touch her cheek and smell her hair, but he couldn't. The realization that his mistrust and suspicion had destroyed their happiness left him numb. They sat and talked about movies and music and Jake and Rocky until early morning when he thumped back down the stairs to go home.

As he rounded the corner of the drugstore he saw Betty Hested riding past on her bicycle. Sweet baby Jesus, I bet that old gal has been cruising Lilly's all night just to see what time I'd leave, he thought as he grimaced a greeting toward Betty and slid into his truck.

THURSDAY, MAY 22

Before you embark on a journey of revenge, dig two graves.

- Confucius

1:00 P

Dan had no idea of the drama waiting for him at the police station the next day. He had expected the chief to be cool and in control, but he was apoplectic. He had expected Lilly to be sitting in the interrogation room looking like hammered whale shit, but she was nonexistent. He had expected Sy to be his usual, taciturn self, but he was lit up like the Vegas strip. He had expected Britta to be smug and self-satisfied, and she didn't disappoint him.

The chief was shouting into the phone, "And you didn't think for a second that the police, who were in the middle of a murder investigation, might be interested?" And then after a pause, "You're joking! Okay, sorry, forget I even called," and with that he stormed out of his office and down the hall to Britta's desk.

"The guy at the ferry terminal says he told you," as his face reddened, his blue eyes became so vivid they seemed to be vibrating.

"I didn't think it was a big deal," Britta shrugged.

"Not a big deal! We were in the middle of a murder investigation. We completely dismissed one suspect because we couldn't place him on the island, and here the whole time, his transportation was hanging off a piling at the ferry terminal, and you were so busy flirting with the primary investigator that you couldn't bother to tell us."

"You're too busy to listen to anything I have to say, anyway."

"Look, Britta, sometimes I'm too busy to listen to you complain about how messy Arne leaves the front desk, but I think I would have found time to discuss the pivotal piece of information in a murder investigation," the chief gave her one last chance to apologize.

"Well, I told Nige about it." She looked him straight in the eyes.

With that one last nudge, the chief became calm. "Britta, I think you'd better start looking for another job."

"Don't blame it on me just because you can't solve your own investigations," Britta shot at his back as she slammed open a drawer and began throwing lipsticks and hand creams into her purse. "And besides, I quit. Nigel's getting me a job as a dispatcher in Juneau!" And with that, she pulled herself up to her full five feet, one inch and squalled out of the police station.

After a short, stunned silence, the chief looked at Dan and said, "Huh, Nigel and Britta; that's a dream team."

"What's going on, Chief?" Dan kept looking for signs of Lilly or the judge, but neither were around.

"We've got a lot to talk about," the chief headed toward his office. "We had a message waiting for us this morning when I got in. Sounds an awful lot like you went over my head and called Seattle yesterday."

After Britta's bad show, Dan decided the best response was no response. "Well, you were right. We've got a kid named Steve Thompson in the back. His parents are the ones who went down in Dixon Entrance because Nels Dagsen was too busy to give them a tow." The chief leaned back in his seat and stared at the water-stained ceiling tiles. "This Thompson kid came in on the morning jet. We just started questioning him, but he's confessed, waived his rights. He's definitely not your average murderer." The phone began to ring as he shook his head in disbelief, "Seattle PD said he was just sitting there waiting for them when they showed up to question him.

I don't know much more than that at this point." He answered the phone with annoyance.

"Well, I'll be. No, no hard feelings," the chief smiled and rolled his eyes at Dan as the conversation progressed. After a few *sures* and *fines* he slammed the receiver into the cradle and chuckled. "That was the Juneau PD wanting a reference for Britta. They were a little apologetic about stealing her right out from under us like that. So I told them how nicely she's going to fit in up there." He was still shaking his head as he and Dan walked into the break room.

"Evidently the purser at the ferry terminal called us first thing Monday morning. They found a skiff hanging off one of the pilings under the dock, but Britta didn't bother passing the information on. Guess she was too busy flirting with Nigel.

"Arne, how about you go get our guy. I think we're going to talk to him in here where there's more room," the chief said as he brushed imaginary crumbs off the break room table.

The chief filled coffee mugs and started making another pot while Arne went to one of the department's two holding cells and returned with the prisoner, Steve Thompson.

Dan observed him as the chief unlocked the handcuffs and gave him a cup of coffee. He had to agree: the guy looked more like a poster child for antiviolence than a murderer. He carried himself like a military man, but he was soft spoken and reticent. Pale blue eyes blended in with his fair complexion and his light brown hair managed to curl in spite of its length.

After a quick round of introductions, the chief began, "So, we're figuring you murdered Dagsen because of your parents?"

"Yeah, my parents. There was that, but it was mostly because of my sister. My twin sister Neva," Thompson began. He rested his hands, still joined by invisible handcuffs, on the white, scuffed table. "Neva was brain damaged at birth. My umbilical cord was wrapped around her neck. She had the mental development of about a five-year-old." Dan felt more and more sorry for the young man as the story unfolded. His lifeless eyes, his crumpled demeanor. Thompson's parents had been adamant that Neva would always live at home. They would take care of her, and by the time they were too old, Steve would step in. Steve and Neva would stay in the family home and the parents would move to a retirement home so that Neva's routine wouldn't be disrupted. That was the family's goal—to give Neva as much of a normal life as possible—and everything they did worked toward that goal. That was the plan his whole life; it was nonnegotiable.

Thompson was in the military when Nels Dagsen left his parents to die, and Neva was put in a public facility until he got out. Her behavior had become more and more erratic in confinement. When he finally came home from the military, he found his sister medicated to the point of vegetation. She had become violent. "All my life she'd been this sweet little kid. Then I come back and they tell me she's dangerous to herself and others; they won't let me take her home. I couldn't even recognize her, she'd changed so much in three years.

"Then a couple of days after I get home, I'm sorting my mom and dad's paperwork and here's a letter from some guy in Petersburg. He says he was a deckhand on Nels Dagsen's boat and that Dagsen could have saved my mom and dad, but he didn't. I just lost it."

As the interrogation continued, Dan drew more and more contrasts between Steve Thompson and Nels Dagsen. They were absolute opposites in every sense of the word, but the most striking difference was that Thompson was willing to kill for his brain-damaged sister, while Nels Dagsen threw his sister under the bus without a second's hesitation.

"So that's when you decided to kill Dagsen?" the chief asked.

"No, I never decided to kill him." Chair legs scraped on concrete as Thompson tried to get more distance between himself and the officers. "I know this sounds ridiculous, but I was just going to come to Petersburg and tell him what he had done to my family. That he had destroyed more than just two old people. Tell him about my sister." He put his head in his hands and ran long, slender fingers through his hair.

The group waited until he sat upright and then the chief continued, "So you came to Petersburg?"

"Huh, no I came to Wrangell," he pronounced it with the accent on the second syllable. "I couldn't get into Petersburg, the jets were all booked, so I just got a ticket as close to Petersburg as I could get. I figured I could drive the rest of the way," he said, shaking his head at his own ignorance.

"I bet those travel plans threw a monkey wrench in the trip," the chief couldn't help but smile at Thompson's ill-conceived reasoning. "So then when you couldn't drive, you rented a skiff?"

"Yeah, I wasn't thrilled about the idea, but the guy said it was easy to get here. 'Straight shot,' he said. He just didn't mention about the tide and not tying skiffs to pilings."

"You wouldn't be the first person to make that mistake." The chief explained the problem to Thompson; if he had tied the skiff up to something that rose and fell with the tide, like the float, he wouldn't have had a problem.

"But let's back up some. You got to Petersburg, and tied the skiff to a piling at the ferry terminal. And then what?"

"Well, I just walked around town. I had no idea I was walking into the middle of this Norwegian thing. I mean I've been to Ballard for their Seventeenth of May Festival, but I didn't know Petersburg was a Norwegian town. I saw those Vikings carrying people off to the bars, and I didn't want to wind up in the middle of something like that. I needed some place to lay low. I saw that little museum and thought that would at least get me out of the rain, so I poked around in there for a while."

"And got dogged by the docent," the chief said.

"She wouldn't leave me alone. I didn't want to be rude. So I signed the guest book, and then I saw this old fishing hook and it said it had been donated by somebody named Dagsen, so I just took it." He leaned back, looking considerably more like the subject of a Norman Rockwell painting, than a calculating killer. "I don't know why I did it. Then I started worrying about the woman noticing it was gone, so I was going to put it back, but people kept coming through. I wasn't worried about getting caught stealing it, but then I was afraid I was going to get caught putting it back.

"I figured I'd better just leave, so I walked down the hill and poked around town for hours. By then the Vikings were so drunk I figured I could dodge them. But I was soaked and freezing." It wasn't hard to imagine how the military man, freshly back from Afghanistan, would be miserable in the forty degree rain of a Petersburg spring day.

"So how did you steal the gun from the Fishing Co-op?" the chief prodded.

"God what a fluke that was," Thompson returned to his story. He had been going from business to business trying to stay out of the rain. FC hardware was the very last store at the very end of town. He'd looked at marine hardware for a couple of hours, then, right when he had started thinking he should just take the skiff back to Wrangell and go home, he noticed a flight of stairs in the back that went to a second floor.

"I was freezing cold and exhausted, and the second floor was really warm. I found a recliner up there all set up for display, and I just settled in and took a nap. It's crazy, but it was the best nap I've ever had," Thompson said. By the time he woke up, the store was closed, but the gun cabinet was wide open. "I thought those guns were some kind of sign. I figured I'd grab one and just use it to scare Dagsen if I ever found him." He crouched behind the counter and took his time picking out a handgun and ammo, and then just walked out the back door as if he owned the place.

"Yeah, we try not to make things too difficult for prospective murderers," Dan was starting to realize what Thompson's story meant. Lilly was off the hook, and his frenetic behavior had been vindicated. The nightmarish aspects of the last few days were already starting to morph into a funny story to tell Rocky when he got off the jet. The chief was smiling appreciatively at his comment. Life was back in order. "Hey, Steve, what kind of shoes do you wear?" Dan continued.

"Man, I can't remember what they're called. I got them at a mall in Qatar, if you can believe that. The guy at the shop told me they were what everyone in America was wearing, and I kind of thought wearing them would make me feel normal—a little closer to home." He reached down and took off a brown leather shoe that he placed gently on the table. Dan turned it over and inspected the same oddly patterned sole from Jake's molds of Stadsvold Trail.

"Well, I'll be," the chief said with admiration. "Jake was right on with those darn tracks of his."

"Yeah Dan, you should have been in charge of this case." Arne's bright orange flannel shirt and red checked hunting hat added a festive touch to the room. "We didn't need Eckles for a damn thing." Equilibrium was restored.

"Ah, yeah Arne, let's not mention Eckles," the chief grimaced. The only subdued occupant was Steve Thompson. The chief looked at him and said, "I guess we'd better get back to your story, Steve."

"It seemed like everything was just choreographed for me," he said. "I know that's not rational, but at the time it seemed to mean something. I was just going from one step to the next without even considering for a second what I was doing," Thompson shrugged his shoulders in resignation and looked from one man to the next for affirmation.

"When I left the hardware store, the streets were pretty much empty, but I could hear music from a few blocks away." Thompson followed the music down to the Sons of Norway and debated whether or not he should go in. "There were so many people coming and going, I thought heck, Dagsen might be there. I might actually find him." He went into the Fish-o-Rama and sat in a corner to people watch. "And then this kind of short, nice looking guy comes in, and he's kind of strutting around like a rooster thinking he owns the place. I knew right away it was him." Dan and Sy exchanged glances. Dan could imagine exactly how Nels would have been working the dinner. "When I heard someone call him Nels, I just kept an eye on him and followed him out when he left."

"When did you start thinking you'd shoot him?" the chief asked.

"I never thought I'd shoot him." Thompson put his head in his hands for several beats and looked again at the men for affirmation. "I followed him down that board street and then shouted to him. He turned around with this big grin on his face like there was nothing better than having somebody out-of-control yelling at him." The group waited while Thompson composed himself and then continued in a shaking voice. "He wouldn't take me seriously, he was laughing at me. And then when he saw that halibut hook, he wigged out. I was trying to tell him about people, but all he could think about was that crazy hook." Tears were streaming down Thompson's cheeks as he wiped his nose on his sleeve and continued, "I took out the gun to get his attention, but he just kept laughing at me." He stopped again, fighting to regain control.

"Then he kind of flipped his hand like I was a fly, and he said I was 'some kind of nut case.' I wanted him to actually listen to me. To hear me, but my words, my sister, my family—it was all nothing to him." Thompson paused to regain control.

Dan nodded encouragement; he understood exactly how Thompson felt.

"I just took the gun out to scare him." His words began sputtering and jerking like a manual transmission in the hands of a novice driver. "I was shaking out of control, and I couldn't believe I started crying and he just kept laughing and then he said, 'You don't even know how to use a gun' so I took the safety off, and the gun just jumped in my hand. I looked up at him and he had this really surprised look on his face. I didn't know what to do. I shot again and, dragged him into the weeds, and then I started running."

The chief watched Thompson sob uncontrollably for a moment and then said, "Okay, Steve, you need to relax. We'll take a little break. Let's get some lunch." Dan called the Past Time for BLTs and pie, and the men waited for Thompson to get himself under control.

The quiet amplified the buzzing of the florescent lights and finally Dan broke the silence: "I'm really sorry about your sister, Steve."

He was thinking of his own family and how difficult life was without the extra complications that the Thompsons had been forced to deal with. Steve Thompson really didn't have any family left at this point. After twenty years as part of a close-knit family, he was adrift. And he had the extra burden of trying to adjust to life after Afghanistan.

Dan wondered if Thompson wouldn't be able to plead some kind of post-traumatic stress and began discussing the possibilities with Sy. After a few minutes he included Steve Thompson in the discussion and then turned the talk around to Afghanistan and Thompson's experiences there. "My youngest son is coming in from Afghanistan on the afternoon jet," he told Thompson. "I bet he'll want to come up and visit as soon as he hears you're here."

The oppression in the room had lifted considerably by the time the men resumed their questioning.

"So you pitched the gun when you got to the Middle Harbor?" the chief pressed the record button as he asked the question.

"Yeah, like I said, everything just unfolded for me. I couldn't go toward the main road or toward the alley, I was afraid someone would see me, so I went toward the harbor. I dropped the gun in the water as soon as I could. I wasn't trying to get rid of evidence, I was just trying to get it away from me. I was horrified that I'd killed a man. Then I ran along the harbor out to the ferry terminal to get the skiff." He laughed when he talked about the missing skiff. At first he thought it had been stolen, then he saw the faint shadow of a hull under water and realized what had happened. "Everything I touch turns to shit." He shook his head in resignation.

"But the crazy thing was, there was a ferry just getting ready to leave. Everybody was standing around watching it, so I walked over to this van that was lined up to board and got in the back. I went from one step to the next like I was dreaming or something. I kept thinking, okay, this is where someone will stop me, but no one did. Dagsen was right, I really was crazy by that time; I kind of started thinking I was being protected by some supernatural force." After Thompson got in the back of the van, he covered himself with a blue tarp and fell asleep. When he heard the purser announce Juneau, he hopped out of the back and blended in with the walk-on passengers. He laughed as he told them the ultimate irony of the trip: "I went out to the main road and started hitching into town from the ferry terminal, and the Fuglvogs, the owners of the van I'd been hiding in, picked me up and gave me a ride to the airport."

"Well, that explains how you got from Wrangell to Juneau without leaving a trail," the chief said. The questioning continued, but Dan asked for permission to go pick up his son at the airport. "The timing couldn't be better," the chief stood and slapped Dan on the back. "Take a few days off and enjoy your boys."

As he reached the door, he turned and looked at Steve Thompson: "So, I'll bring both boys back to talk if you're still in town tonight. They'll want to hear where you were stationed in Afghanistan."

Dan ran the entire gamut of emotions as he raced home to pick up Jake. A thick cloud of fog had rolled in, and he was afraid Rocky's jet would overfly, winding up in Juneau or Anchorage.

Different options for connecting with Rocky if the jet overflew ran through one part of Dan's mind, while the intricacies of the murder occasionally interrupted like a schist of quartz in sedimentary rock. The main gist of this second train of thought was the fact that Lilly was no longer a murder suspect. And along with that thought came the realization that his feelings for Lilly really had clouded his judgment during the investigation. Shit, what the hell was I thinking? He wondered.

2:00 P

The airport was quiet, but the town had clearly been busy. Several people waved and grinned at their old friend Dan Fields. Harry Baker, the permit broker, came over and pumped his hand as he walked into the terminal. "Glad to hear you got Nels' murderer behind bars. Everybody knew you could handle it," he said with a slap on the back.

"Shit, Harry, that slap is going to leave a welt," Jake said. Just as Harry Baker was predicting an over-flight, the jet came lofting through the clouds, each wingtip trailing a feathery mist. The jet landed with a teeth-cracking bounce and taxied the length of the runway while the anticipation in the terminal bloomed. Everyone erupted in laughter as Rocky, the first person off the jet, raced down the ramp, jumped in the air and threw a fist toward the sky. He jogged through the terminal and hugged his dad and brother fiercely. "So are the hooters boomin'?"

Hooters, or grouse, were one of the men's favorite hunts, and the boys had been chasing the noisy little birds every spring for years. "Oh, they're booming alright, but instead of hooting, they're calling your name!" Jake beamed.

"I wouldn't expect anything less," Rocky said after a second round of bear hugs.

The past is never dead. It's not even past.

William Faulkner

2:00 P

The three men were sitting in the sun on the deck, gazing through the cedars at the Wrangell Narrows in the distance. The scent of skunk cabbage blended subtly with the wood smoke. Father and sons sat with a beer in one hand and a single, humble grouse at their feet. "You're such a flipping idiot," Jake was laughing and punching Rocky in the arm.

"I got a hooter, didn't I? So how many hooters *you* having for dinner tonight?" Rocky feinted and returned the jab.

"You just about killed yourself," Jake dodged.

"Yeah, but I would have died happy. And you could have buried me with the hooter."

"Are you kidding? We would have buried you and eaten the hooter."

Hooters provide a unique hunting experience. They perch in a tree and rely on protective coloration to conceal them from hunters.

Unfortunately for them, the little guys don't have the sense to keep quiet. They maintain a constant hoot or "boom" that directs the hunters to their exact location.

They had hiked and struggled through ankle tangle for more than an hour trying to locate this particular bird. They finally found the tree, but the grouse wasn't visible from the ground. Dan had tried to "cluck him down," imitating a female grouse to get the male to leave his perch, but that had just resulted in a lot of jibes from his boys, who didn't believe he could actually do it and accused their father of trying to catch the grouse "with his pants down."

Rocky wasn't going to let a bird get the best of him, so he climbed a neighboring tree, going higher and higher until he could finally see it. He was so far up the tree, though, that the kick from his gun sent the tree top swaying back and forth with Rocky yelling, "Whoa, whoa Nellie!" at the top of his lungs leaving, Jake laughing uncontrollably, and Dan yelling, "Hold on! Hold on, Son!" The entire scene had looked a little like an Elmer Fudd and Bugs Bunny routine.

"There's no way I was going to leave that little shyster up there taunting us. I didn't come back from Afghanistan to sit around and let a chicken get the best of me." The three men heard the sound of a car throwing gravel and waited curiously until they saw Lilly pull up in her ancient Subaru. The vehicle had met a light pole head-on at some point in its brutal existence, and it seemed to be echoing its driver's grin as it rolled to a stop next to Dan's wood pile.

"I can't believe that thing made it all the way up here!" Dan said with a laugh.

"If there's a beer at the end of the road, it can usually make the trip," Lilly said as she gave Rocky a hug. "I may have dropped a couple of parts on the way up, but I'll grab them on the way down."

Jake went to get Lilly a beer as she settled in next to Rocky with a smile. "Is that a beer? You're not old enough to drink."

"Yeah, I am," Rocky laughed. "I turned twenty-one in Afghanistan, but it's not legal for soldiers to buy alcohol over there, so I had to get an eight-year-old kid to buy for me." The whole group laughed as the conversation moved toward the murder.

"So it was family after all, huh?" Lilly said as she savored the sunshine.

"Yeah, just not the family everybody thought. I'm willing to wager that poor kid is going to spend the best part of his life in jail for it, too," Dan replied.

"It should be justifiable. If someone messed with you I'd go after them," Rocky said.

His father smiled. "If something happened to you or Jake? I don't know what I'd do. You know you spend your whole life working toward a Harley or a big house or an African hunting trip. And then something like this happens and you realize: there's nothing out there, not a single thing that matters except your family."

Dan leaned back, turning his head toward the sun. "On a day like today it's pretty easy to forget the Burg's downsides and just marvel at how gorgeous everything is." The whole group sat for a moment gazing over the tree tops to where a tiny tug was towing a Lego-like barge up the Wrangell Narrows. "It can rain for three months straight, and then we have one day like today and I forget it all." The sun warmed the cedar deck radiating a comfortable heat.

After the fear and alienation of the investigation the entire group had a new appreciation for each other. "I probably shouldn't admit it, but I always thought you boys were part of my family. When I was younger I thought I was going to marry your dad, and when I didn't have kids of my own, I figured I had the right to adopt you two."

"That was fine with us. Especially after Mom left." Rocky said. Then after a pause, he added, "What? What did you punch me for?"

"Well, since we're not even going to try to be subtle," Jake shook his head, "I punched you because we were just going inside, or for a hike, or to get more beer or something."

"Oh, I get it!" and with that the two boys jumped to their feet and headed to Jake's truck.

~~~

Sitting in a companionable silence, Dan and Lilly watched them leave.

"I hope Steve Thompson will get off on post-traumatic stress disorder. I think he's already suffered enough," Lilly said to break the ice.

"I don't know if that's going to happen. He spent a long time trying to cover his trail. He managed to finagle a birth certificate for David Leventer, a friend of his who died when they were in elementary school, and he got himself a whole set of fake I.D. That took a lot of time and a lot of planning. It's going to be hard to say the murder wasn't premeditated. And the second shot. Even if the first one was an accident, that doesn't explain why he shot twice, or why he got ammo for the gun in the first place. I suspect he'll be going away for a long time, but it doesn't seem like he even cares."

"He was thinking of his family. I can't believe Nels left that couple out there just to get to an opening," Lilly said softly.

"I'm sorry this has been so hard on you, Lil."

"You know, it's been hard in some ways, but it's been kind of liberating, too. I was tied to Petersburg because of my family and friends, and now I feel like I can actually start my life."

"So now what? Do you have to go to court about the estate?"

"We're getting a lawyer, but we don't need to go to court. We're kind of having the opposite problem. Everyone's saying, 'You take the money. No you take the money.'" Lilly laughed. "Meera and Anya have gotten pretty friendly in the last few days." She beamed.

"We've agreed that I'll get half the estate and then Meera and Anya are going to split the other half. We're all going to invest part of the money in Anya's boutiques. Meera's cousin is a leather worker in the Philippines, so she is going to set up production and put the whole family to work making boots and purses to sell at Anya's dress shops."

Dan laughed at Lilly's enthusiasm. "But what about you? Are you going to start making shoes and purses with Meera?"

"No, I'm going to be a silent partner. Anya is going to run the retail business, Meera is going to run the production side, and I'm going to college. I figure it's about time."

"Lilly, that's great," Dan's excitement showed from his crinkled eyes to his toothy grin.

"I've spent over forty years of my life in Petersburg, Alaska. I think it's time to see a little more of the country. I'm going to apply to University of Washington. They have a strong special education department, and that's what I'm looking for." Her smile broadened as she added, "And I already have a summer job."

"What are you doing this summer?"

"I've been hired by Derek Aaronson to babysit his girls while he's out fishing. I'm finally getting a little bit of a family. I've already picked out blueprints for a little house. Nothing fancy. Just a place I can take care of the girls and stay during the summers."

"So you're not going to write Petersburg off entirely?"

"No way. People did what they thought was right for Nels. You can't blame them for that." She paused uncomfortably for a moment and then looked at Dan and said, "You're the only person I don't want to leave behind. These last few days have been awful, but having your friendship again after all those years made it so much easier."

"Well, then, maybe, I've got some good news for you." He paused for effect before he smiled and said, "I'm heading to Seattle too."

"What? What about your job? And the boys?"

Dan explained his change of plans. He had gone into the station on Friday and put in his two weeks' notice. The chief acted disappointed, but Dan suspected he was really relieved. He had ignored the chief's leadership during the investigation, and he knew he would do it again if that was what his conscience dictated. As Jake said, he was uncoachable.

Lilly took a more self-centered view of the situation. "You quit because of me? Danny, I'm so sorry."

"No, it's not your fault, Lil. And besides, Jake's going in on Monday to apply for the position. The chief loved those prints he did. And they were both in the Screaming Eagles in the military. He's a perfect fit."

Lilly laughed. "Jake's just as hard headed as you are. That won't help any."

"Yeah, he's definitely hard headed, but if the chief hires Jake, it won't be controversial. If he doesn't work out, the chief won't take the heat for it, like he would with me."

"Well, I guess that's great for Jake, but what about you?"

"You promise you won't flip me any shit?"

"No, I'm not promising you anything."

"Earl Sanderson has a power troll permit he hasn't used in years. I'm going to line up a boat and Earl and I are going out trolling. For long periods of time. Until he's off the Aquavit."

"Seriously?"

"Very seriously." Dan saw the old timer at the liquor store, and Earl made the proposal. Although Dan initially said no, he changed his mind when he started giving the idea some thought. Earl was close to Dan's dad's age and his failing liver was going to be the end of him if he didn't stop drinking. And, he had a wealth of knowledge and history he could share with Dan out on the boat.

Dan had finally agreed on the condition that they worked with a doctor for the first few weeks. Now he was actually looking forward to the job. "Earl won't be the first guy to use fishing to sober up. He's sworn off Aquavit and switched over to beer already, and he started AA meetings last night. We've got a doctor's appointment tomorrow."

Lilly gazed out at the water for a moment. "I thought you might be going to Seattle."

"Well, Earl is the short-term plan. That should get me through the summer. Then there's the long-term plan. Dave Versteeg owes me a favor; he's in charge of personnel for the barge line and he said I can walk right into the first position that opens up on a tug. I guess there's a couple of old guys who'll be retiring pretty soon, so I'll power troll and work on Jake's house until something opens up. When it does, I'll be working out of Seattle."

"Uff da. You've got everything lined out," Lilly said, as she leaned forward and wrapped both arms around her knees to hide her smile.

"It-sha. That I have."

"All right Dan Fields. I want a straight answer and I want it now." Lilly was suddenly back to business. "Ever since we were in elementary school, every time I said *uff da*, you said *it sha* back to me. I thought it was the Norwegian answer to *uff da*, so when I went to Norway, I used it, but they had no idea what I was talking about. Had never heard the word before. So then I asked everyone I met in Sweden. Same thing. Never heard of it. This has gone on for close to forty years. I want to know what *it sha* means. I swear you're the only person in the world who says it."

Dan watched this outburst, first with confusion and then with amusement. "I'll be go to hell, Lilly, you are so damn clueless sometimes. So, you want to know the translation of *it sha*, huh?" He waited for her nod before he continued, "It's pig-Latin for shit."

It took a moment to absorb his translation. Then she wound up and gave him a substantial punch in the gut. "You're a jerk," she laughed at her own foolishness. Dan used the punch to grab her arm and pull her closer. "I can't believe how natural this feels after all those years," she said several minutes later. "But now what?"

"First, we've got twenty-five years of movies we need to get caught up on." Dan squeezed her tighter. "You can't imagine the number of times I watched a movie and wished I was watching it with you."

A raven danced a celebration on the deck railing.